rundown

Also by Michael Cadnum

rundown

by michael cadnum

"Funded by
LSTA Young Adult Grant"

VIKING

VIKING

Published by the Penguin Group
Penguin Putnam Books for Young Readers,
345 Hudson Street, New York, New York 10014, U.S.A.
Penguin Books Ltd, 27 Wrights Lane, London W8 5TZ, England
Penguin Books Australia, Ltd, Ringwood, Victoria, Australia
Penguin Books Canada Ltd, 10 Alcorn Avenue, Toronto, Ontario, Canada M4V 3B2
Penguin Books (N.Z.) Ltd, 182-190 Wairau Road, Auckland 10, New Zealand

Penguin Books Ltd, Registered Officer: Harmondsworth, Middlesex, England

First published in 1999 by Viking,
a division of Penguin Putnam Books for Young Readers

10 9 8 7 6 5 4 3 2

LIBRARY OF CONGRESS CATALOGING-IN-PUBLICATION DATA
Cadnum, Michael.
Rundown / by Michael Cadnum.   99B7886
      p.   cm.
Summary: As a game, sixteen-year-old Jennifer pretends that she has been
attacked by a serial rapist, but then she finds herself getting more attention
than she wanted, from the police and her parents.
ISBN 0-670-88377-8
[1. Honesty—Fiction.   2. Rape—Fiction.   3. Criminal investigation—Fiction.
4. Parent and child—Fiction.]   I. Title.
PZ7.C11724Ru   1999   [Fic]—dc21   98-49554   CIP   AC

Printed in U.S.A.
Set in Stempel Garamond

for Sherina

A spider
in the rain—
so still

rundown

chapter 1

One month before my sister's wedding I did a terrible thing.

I had picked the hour with care—twilight, a long summer sunset in Strawberry Canyon. A few joggers plodded ahead of me on the asphalt path that paralleled the road. I was loping along easily, able to keep this pace as long as I wanted. I reached the bend in the road and stopped, my hands on my hips.

I had selected the location with equal care, blackberry bushes dense beside the path, a stand of trees.

The view west of here was luminous blue, the setting sun mirrored off the Pacific, the sky filling with glow. You can take in a great view from the canyon, the gray buildings on the campus, steam from the ducts twisting free in the cool evening air. Until the last moment I told myself I didn't have to do this today, I didn't have to do it at all.

I let the joggers slog their way back down the path, determined to burn off their four hundred and eighty calories an hour, and cheating a little, getting help from the downhill slope. One of the guys caught my glance. I knew what he took in was easy on the eyes, a sixteen-year-old in shorts and an oversize gray Cal sweatshirt, sleeves scissored at the elbows, bra strap showing at one shoulder. I have a healthy appearance, even with my hair jammed under a watch cap, not dazzling like Cassandra, but okay.

I gave him a blank look and let my eyes show null interest, like the guy was so much empty space. But he was already past me, the white soles of his running shoes flashing down the growing dark. An animal, belly low to the road, flashed from dark to dark, one of the feral cats that haunt the hills, pets gone wild.

I began to be a little afraid.

The recent news had been jammed with stories about the South Bay rapist, seven assaults in sixteen days, his composite face on Channel Two news every night, and here I was, the cool air stealing up through the bay trees along the path, the blackberry vines black scribbles.

I didn't have to go through with this, I told myself, running in place, dancing a little to stay loose, not wanting to be stranded out here in the dark. It was filling up with night, the canyon, car headlights lancing up the road, giving me a faceful of glare.

In their passage the twilight was all the darker, and the game I was ready to play felt real.

I don't keep secrets from myself, so the state of my nerves surprised me. Something stirred the bush beside me—a random breeze or a sparrow in a hurry to find refuge.

I decided to get it over with.

I let my body do a stunt roll into the blackberries, holding my breath against the scratching of the thorns. And then I tumbled, not able to stop myself. I had anticipated most of this, and wanted it, the branches scrabbling, clinging, brambles snagging, breaking, but then my own weight carried me downward too fast, the wiry coils of thorns not strong enough to bear me. I pitched down, hard, into the dry creek.

Dust has a smell—dry, cloying, as it rises up around your body. The bad light showed berry stains on my hands, and long fine tears where the thorns had clung, the deepest points beading with blood.

I steeled myself and fought upward, clawing at the earth though the maze of brambles, snatching at cutting points, wrestling through the brush.

And through, out onto the path.

I hit the traffic sign there beside the road with the side of my hand. The sign gave a loud metallic bang, screw heads rattling. The sign was a vivid yellow diamond with a black arrow, letting motorists know a curve was just ahead. It vibrated for a long time, humming with the force of my blow, because I had hit it hard—it was part of my plan.

By then I was breathing audibly, gulping air, and I stepped back into the brambles for a second, because it wasn't a plan anymore. I heard someone.

I listened.

I was playing this just a little too well, the way Cassandra did in that play she wrote herself about having an abortion, weeping tears so you thought she was feeling something. You could sense the audience, heads together, amazed and anguished, wondering, Christ, how could someone so young have such compassion?

Someone was out there, trying not to make a sound.

chapter 2

The campus of the University of California, Berkeley, is a landscape of venerable trees and austere multi-story buildings. Vent grills in the pavement give off hot air from somewhere underground, and so do big periscope-like pipes, fuming off a smell of old books and wall plaster, the entire institution breathing.

There was always a university police car parked by Strawberry Creek, where a cute little bridge arched over a feeble pulse of water. But on this night, of all nights, I found only a few spots of grease and a rut worn in the ground near a redwood tree where the rover unit was supposed to park.

Hall lights streamed out from the buildings as after-hours students hurried through the doors. Assistant professors picking up some extra pay teaching summer classes down-geared their bikes as they pumped the slope toward the street. I was breathing shakily and felt a sweaty chill all over my body.

I could still change my mind.

But then a police unit purred along through the indistinct figures of people, taking its time the way only cops do, not going anywhere, wanting criminals and possible victims and taxpayers to see where they are, keeping an eye on the sole skateboarder taking a long, smooth ride into the night.

I had rehearsed this in my mind, but doing it felt like just another fantasy. I beat my hands on the top of the police car. This had been what I had visualized with the greatest intensity, my opening lines.

My first words were supposed to be a stammered communication. I had sent the phrases through a series of mental rewrites. *Tried to rape* sounded wrong, overdramatic, and leading to a discussion of how far the attempt had gone. *Mugged* was out of the question, as though I was a business woman with a purse stuffed with cash.

I wanted the drama of attempted rape, without any lurid and embarrassing details, and I knew exactly how far I would take this. I knew how to fake out my few lines, and what would happen as they called my parents and my parents came and got me, telling me they were glad I was all right—*all right* meaning more than my father could put into words, relief making his voice breathy.

So I was surprised when the car door burst open, the cop already holding a transmitter attached to the dash with a coiling black cord. Later I would try to replay my first words, and I couldn't make them stick together.

I said something about an attacker, Strawberry Canyon,

and I think I used the phrase, "I barely got away." The word *barely* would haunt me that night, slipping into sentences where it didn't belong.

"Are you hurt?" he was asking.

A mock-gold nameplate over his badge gave his name, but I couldn't register letters right then. I had planned something less hurried. I had a description worked up over recent days, based on news reports and posters stapled to trees all over the Bay Area.

The rectangular nameplate above his badge read *Fountain*, like an ad for sparkling drinking water, or some holy place. Officer Fountain was alight with excitement and reassurance, a rookie or a cop bored with rousting drunks from Sproul Plaza. I told him the attacker was about this tall, indicating a height with my throbbing hand, about six feet, a good five inches taller than me. "With a ski mask," I said, "and—"

I made a feeble gesture up and down my front. "A zipper jacket," Officer Fountain prompted.

I nodded.

"Dark blue?" he was asking, and I could hear the thrill under the terse just-the-facts note in his voice.

The cop talked into the side of his hand, a fit, muscular, woolly individual, stuffed into his uniform, proof what a pass to the staff gym can do. He had the back door of the police cruiser open, talking into his radio, using the tough monotone of cops and airline pilots, saying he had a possible two-sixty-one, subject at large.

"You sure you have no injuries to report?" asked Officer Fountain.

I was all set for a little paperwork and then a wait for

my parents to get back from the opera fund-raiser. I'd sit red-eyed and brave in the university police headquarters, calling Bernice Heath, the housekeeper, and maybe letting her do a mommy hen act. Maybe this deep-chested Officer Fountain would hang around to hold my hand, literally, if I played the courage routine just so.

And then act two, Dad and Mom flushed with just-under-the-legal-limit bubbly, chattering about something like why do the organizers bother with paté, it's just flavored fat. Wide-eyed and worried, and wanting to be relieved. My parents would run smack into a big chunk of my life, little Jennifer, daughter number two, the one who isn't Cassandra.

I was content for the moment to sit in the back seat of the police unit, the radio crackling with university cops, their voices stepping on each other, the female dispatcher barely able to acknowledge each transmission with a hurried nine-oh-nine, cop code for "heard and understood."

Even as the officer drove me up Strawberry Canyon and I identified the crime scene, I didn't recognize the excitement for anything but routine police concern. I stayed in the car and directed the policeman's huge flashlight, beam turning the shrubbery silver.

"Not there," I said, not having any trouble sounding disturbed by what was happening. "Right there." A gap in the berry vines.

I had studied the police and chosen university law enforcement on purpose, keen to avoid falling into the hands of Oakland or Berkeley cops with their crime labs and reporters hanging around the desk sergeant. I had monitored cop calls on my dad's old Radio Shack shortwave.

But it was only as we left the crime scene and cruised down Bancroft Avenue that I had a sickening sensation.

The street was populated with people on their way to drink coffee and listen to Mozart in one of the music stores, and with one part of my mind I thought like any crime victim would have, envying all these normal, idle graduate students, an easy class schedule during the summer months, nothing to do but smoke French cigarettes and look intellectual.

In another frantic command post of my psyche I was aware than we were putting the campus behind us, traveling fast, the chrome of the window frame flashing off and on with the car's emergency blinkers.

We pulled off Martin Luther King, Jr., Way into the parking lot of a place that resembled a bargain-rate motel, an aluminum-framed, prefabricated assembly of offices, the city police department.

chapter 3

Each cop wore a crisp khaki short-sleeved shirt and a toy-store badge, a bright nickel star, *Berkeley Police* in black.

They wore their handguns high on their hips, where it would be hard to get at the weapons without making an effort. A solicitous sergeant took down the number of my dad's cell phone, jotted my address, and made a solemn, silent *oh* of surprise when I spelled my last name, the one he had no doubt heard on the radio and seen in the gourmet section of the supermarket, my dad's idealized signature, *Terry Thayer,* on bottles of salad dressing.

Then they parked me in a side chair, after I said I didn't need to "talk to someone right away," meaning, I gathered, a counselor.

The police department hummed like a bank five minutes before closing, and I took some comfort in the fact that my case was not causing armed men and women to rush out into the night.

I was getting used to this, telling myself I had done fairly well, when I sensed someone close to me, leaning over me. I gave one of those you-startled-me laughs.

She gave me a down-turned smile of apology. "I'm Detective Margate," she said, "with the Sex Crimes Detail." She indicated a doorway in the distance with a movement of her head.

She led me into a small office with a window, a view of night sky and parking lot.

A man stood up as I entered, closing a folder, moving newspaper off a comfy-looking padded chair on wheels. She said, "This is Detective Ronert."

Detective Ronert smiled, kind, nonthreatening, plainly well schooled at victim psychology. He moved the chair into the corner.

"How are you feeling, Jennifer?" Detective Margate was asking. "Can we get you a glass of water?"

We kept quiet while Detective Ronert left, and I sat in the chair, putting my elbows on the padded arms. I liked being here in the corner, a wall on either side of me.

He came back with an incredibly small paper cup with pleats in it. All three of us waited while I drank the water, one mouthful. Detective Margate was a tall woman with dark, short hair and black eyebrows that gave her a piercing look, like a bird that kills small animals.

"We're here to help you through this," said Detective Margate, giving me a straight smile this time, no apology. "In any way we can."

"I want to go home."

She could turn the smile on, and turn it off. "We'll just ask you a couple of questions," she said. She touched the side of my neck gently, where a thorn slash stung. "What are these?"

"Blackberry bushes," I said. I meant that the marks were the effect of blackberry thorns in violent contact with my skin, but something about Detective Margate made my brain freeze.

"Does your hand hurt?" she asked.

The side of my hand was already sunrise-blue; I bruise easily. "Not very much."

"Can you open your fingers?"

I opened my hand, shut it.

She wiggled her fingers, a duchess giving a silent *'bye for now.* She wore a dark chocolate-brown tweed jacket with blue houndstooth checks, a white blouse, and a dark navy blue skirt, the same sort of plainclothes look nuns wore when they used to drop by my dad's restaurant for his yearly donation of gourmet fare. I wiggled my fingers back at her.

She held out a forefinger, and I sat still, puzzled, while she pressed a knuckle against the cutoff sleeve of my sweatshirt. An ant trickled down off the cloth under her hand.

She leveled her bird-of-prey eyes at me. "Tell me what happened, Jennifer."

I watched the ant hesitating on the whorl of her pale knuckle. "Nothing happened."

She was about to ask, so I added quickly, "Nothing sexual."

"Let's start with what he *did* do," she said, then she

lifted the ant to her lips, and blew, gently, the ant hanging on, but crumpling with effort, losing the fight. The ant vanished.

"He barely touched me," I said.

Detective Margate was writing on a sheet of paper on a clipboard, the white pen making a whisper across the page. She glanced up, and her dark brown eyes bore into me. "Where?"

I lifted my shoulder meaningfully, let it fall. "We need the camera," she told Detective Ronert. "Did he touch you anywhere else?"

"I want to go home," I said, "and forget it happened." Detective Ronert fumbled in a black canvas bag, unzipping compartments, prying off a lens cap.

Detective Margate's voice was soft without being gentle, a woman used to giving orders without having to repeat herself. "It's very important, Jennifer, that you tell us if he touched you in any intimate part of your body."

"He touched me on my shoulder. He grabbed me," I corrected myself.

She nodded reassuringly, but I could hear the questions stacking up. For a crazy instant I thought I might be in trouble for protecting myself from an assailant. "He caught me from behind, I turned around and hit him, and then he pushed me into the bushes."

I'm built, as Dad would say. I'm not fat, but I'm not slender. If I stop running for a couple of days I tend to put on four pounds. You could see the detective imagining me giving this criminal a fist to the face. And believing it.

She wrote for a few moments. "Was he wearing gloves?" she asked.

My mind did a racing data search, recalling what I knew about the series of attacks up and down Alameda County. "Leather gloves," I said. "Tight fitting."

She handed me a sheet, nice and crisp, not staple-punished and bent out of shape from being wrapped around a redwood tree. It was a police-artist composite, one of those ovals that look like a face without resembling a human. One of the victims had seen her attacker before he tugged the dark knit head-covering down over his features. AGE 25–35, WEIGHT 140–150, a white male, skinny for his height.

The shame of what I was doing shook me—swept through me, a physical force that rattled the paper in my hands. Women had been brutalized by this assailant, and here I was, turning his crime into a trashy piece of theater.

But even as this feeling silenced me I could tell that to an observer, even an experienced one, my feelings could be misjudged.

"Let me see if I'm picturing this correctly," she said, offering me her all-pro, easy-on smile. "The perpetrator runs after you, puts his hand on you. Like this?" She acted out a slow-motion charade, a mummy trying out for football, her right arm outstretched. "He seized your shoulder, you wheeled, and—"

"Hit him," I said, my voice nearly silent.

I should not have used the phrase *hit him* twice. It sounded insistent.

But the detective made a noncop remark. "You should be able to go out running without someone assaulting you." She was speaking as a citizen, as a woman, although you could tell that a rape from a notorious attacker would have been important, getting her name in the news. As it was, my incident was not very important, and maybe some disappointment peppered the detective's relief.

"I was lucky."

"You were lucky, but you were still the victim of assault with intent. Did you observe anything about his person that you could identify?"

"Scars?"

"The color of his eyes, a limp. Anything about his carriage—the way he stood and moved."

I knew what *carriage* meant; I was a tiny bit irritated. Also, I was afraid I was going to let her down. I offered, "He said something."

"What?"

Jesus, what did he say?

I hated myself for ad-libbing. I cleared my throat, really wanting that water now. "I could barely hear him."

"What did he say?"

"He said, 'Wait a minute.'"

Detective Ronert held a Pentax camera up to his face, and the flash caught me looking. I blinked. He was one of those men who can't help getting a little fat; he probably starved himself, ate nothing but celery for lunch. He had a thick neck and pink face, his whole person buoyant, the hair on his head thin on top. He squinted, snapped another shot, the entire room flash-frozen.

"Do you think you could recognize his voice," said Detective Margate, "if you heard it again?"

I felt my mind hunt the possible answers, weighing the

strength of each. If I said no, how much would it weaken my story? Maybe I wanted my story to collapse. This was as good a time as any to blurt the truth.

I said, "I might."

"Get a picture of these," said Detective Margate, running her finger over a prize set of scratches on my forearm. "And here," she said, pointing to my bra strap.

Both detectives examined my shoulder, and I tried to let my mind wander far away from this, the camera focusing on a bruise. The camera whined between snaps, the automatic flash leaving violet smears on my vision.

chapter 4

My dad hurried toward the office wearing a tux, his long silk opera scarf trailing, about to fall free. My mother was close behind, in her new William Calvert evening dress, gray so dark it was same-as-black. Her blond hair had that artfully swept-back look she pays for on Maiden Lane, her hair consultant as fussy as a surgeon.

Both my parents had a taut, pale look, afraid of bad news, and I quailed inside, not feeling the way I had expected at all.

I took his hands. I told him I was all right, emphasizing the words, giving them the right weight, the right eye contact, and he walked me a few steps away from the chair, reading my eyes, like someone guiding me out for the last dance.

"I just want to go home and pretend this never happened," I said, partly because it was becoming more and more true, and partly because it was the most normal thing I could think of saying.

He closed his eyes, too shaken to give voice to his "Thank God," the words just visible on his lips.

My mother began to put her hand on my shoulder, but then ended up with an airy, half embrace, holding back, and then stepping all the way back, ashen. I couldn't keep myself from flinching when I thought she would touch me where I hurt. She currently worked as an industrial psychologist. She ran a company that designed Silicon Valley job application questionnaires, catching industrial spies and sexual harassers before their names made the payroll.

I had not expected to feel what I did then. These are my parents, I wanted to tell the detectives. These two beautiful people.

My father introduced himself to the detectives and asked to be briefed. My mother walked around the office, corner to corner, her golden hair upswept and kept in place by magic. Detective Margate ran her right hand down the front of her tweed jacket. When her fingers reached the garment's hem, they gave a gentle tug.

My dad has this effect on people. You see him in ads, billboards, television, Wildhorse Ranch, Bloody Russian, Primo Virgin Vinaigrette, his gaze looking out at the shopper, half smile half don't-disappoint-me twinkle.

Detective Ronert offered to get my parents some coffee, "Although it really isn't fit to drink."

"Coffee would be delightful," said my mother. If you didn't know her well you would think she was used to this, standing in a police station dressed like a movie star. She did quick turns around the office, her heels making neat clip-clops. She was a woman of hidden tensions, even after years of therapy and a steady diet of beta blockers. She had studied to be an opera singer years ago, but stage fright had stopped her career.

Detective Margate reprised my account of the crime, referring to a form on her desk, stopping to correct the spelling of a word.

Ronert returned with two cups of coffee in white porcelain cups emblazoned with the Berkeley police insignia, a yellow star framed by the silhouette of a badge. I had to wonder if there were Berkeley police T-shirts and paper plates, for parties with a crime-fighting theme. He left the cups on the desk; no one touched them.

We all listened to Detective Margate. When she was done she arranged some papers on her desk, and my mother ran her hands up and down her arms, like she was cold.

"We're hoping Jennifer can help us," said the detective.

"How?" asked my mother.

"She's the only witness to have heard his voice," said Detective Margate.

"I don't want my daughter being caught up in this," said my mother.

She didn't mean simply that she wanted to undo any crime that had occurred, erase it from our collective memory. She meant this place, these two detectives, these off-green walls.

Something passed between the two women. Detective

Ronert said, "We think tonight's attacker is the same individual. The same perpetrator as the others. He might well still be hiding in the hills."

Detective Margate said, "We'll have dozens of officers out there, beating the brush. Park rangers, too. This might be the night we catch him."

"Of course my family will cooperate in every way," my father said. "If we can help catch this guy—" My father hates to get emotional. He glanced around the room, taking a deep breath.

With something like kindness in her voice, Detective Margate said that she tried his recipe for persimmon pudding last New Year's Eve. "It was wonderful!" she said.

"You use the whole nutmeg, the entire nut, grated, you can't miss," my father said, adjusting the black bow tie, flexing his shoulders, relieved at the change of subject. "You use too much sugar you lose the taste of the fruit." His eyes lit up, and the passion came over him as he spoke, the way he could talk to an airline ticket clerk about mangoes, or run into someone walking his dachshund and end up talking about where to buy the best veal.

Dad's Fine Food Five had started on KSFO a few years before as a stopgap, a way to keep him busy and pull in some dollars after his restaurant burned down. The five minutes once a week had turned into eight minutes every day but weekends. Then Kraft Foods bought his line of salad dressings, which he had started as a hobby tax write-off, four employees in a cinder-block kitchen in Napa. Now he was planning the pilot for a network TV show, and he was on the phone with his tax lawyer every day.

"Did you ever try my crema fritta?" he asked.

You could see Detective Margate wondering if she should tell a polite lie. "No, not yet."

"Or my chilled grape pudding—"

My mother put a hand on the crook of his arm.

But I loved listening to him. And I was suddenly hungry sitting there, eager to be home and having some of those lamb chops in white wine we had in the fridge, unless Bernice had decided the egg and lemon sauce would not bear reheating.

"Before you go I need you to sign this," said Detective Margate.

"What is it?" asked Dad, taking it from her hand. He held it at arm's length, reading. "Incident report." He tried making the name of the form sound funny, on safer ground when he could sound ironic.

He looks like the pictures you see of Napoleon, a fleshy, luminous face and a gaze that tends to be inward, considering. While Napoleon was probably thinking, "The artillery is aiming too high," Dad was usually thinking something like, "Chef should take it easy on the oregano."

I signed my name, realizing as I penned the letters that my signature was a passable copy of my dad's registered-trademark signature, the one a corporation had just bought. So I finished signing my name with a flourish, something new, *Jennifer Thayer* underscored by a diagonal line.

I had been gripping the Bic too hard. I put it down and flexed my fingers.

Then I made a mistake.

My face went blank. It wasn't the shaken, nerveless face

of a victim, but something else—the look of a self-conscious actress, unsure of her role.

"I'm making an appointment for you, Jennifer," said Detective Margate, in a tone of voice I had not heard since my father arrived. "With one of our victim's services counselors."

"We can take care of our daughter," said my mother.

The detective said, "This is an investigation we're conducting." After an emphatic silence, she added, "And we want the best for Jennifer."

Even women make the mistake of thinking that if a person is good looking she can be easily deceived. My mother looks good, and she gets what she wants. She has fired a string of personal secretaries, and when she used to complain about a less than perfect score on Cass's English test, the teacher always changed the grade. It's easy for me to imagine her name on an opera poster, ELIZABETH ESHEL-MANN, MEZZO-SOPRANO.

My father steered me away from the desk, nudged me without touching, his aura pushing my aura.

We stood outside the detective's office and tried to hear what Mom was saying to the police.

chapter 5

In the back seat of the car my mother changed, lost her erect posture and slumped like a boneless thing. Her hand flopped outward, squeezed nothing, found mine.

"That's the one," she said, when I made a tiny intake of air.

The hand I hit him with, she meant.

I made one of those noises people use to affirm a statement, a small sound, not a word.

"Jesus, I'm proud of you, Jennifer," she said. "For fighting like that."

Freeway lights glided by, Dad guiding the brand-new Lincoln at the speed limit.

This was all new to us, including our neighborhood, a domain of ivy-covered gothic four-stories, tucked up against the Berkeley/Oakland city line. It was a few blocks of Jaguars and front-garden fountains, and the biggest fortress in the neighborhood had come on the market the same week Dad quit the radio show.

It was like pulling into the driveway of a stranger, watching the iron gates ease open with a push of the button on the dash. The gate closed behind us, and the engine purred, the tires making that sound I find so comforting, the fine crackle of grit. The garage doors swept open, the headlights bright against the back wall.

And then Dad left the engine running, the parking brake set, none of us wanting to enter the glamorous soundstage of the house, finding sanctuary in a car with nine hundred miles on the odometer.

Our lives had always been a series of choices, travel or a bigger apartment, and we had always picked travel, even when Cassandra said she would die if she had to see Rome again. I knew what she meant, hating it when another elegant three-piece suit pinched Cassandra on the butt.

But even when Cass was at Stanford we scrimped enough to see Italy every summer. Rome is okay, if you can get one of the stringy cats to creep close enough to take anchovy scraps from your fingers, but we always had to go in the summer, when we were off school. It was hot, and motor scooters are everywhere in Rome, women in elegant one-pieces and fanny-pinchers in Armani suits flying from all directions.

But my parents were happiest together when they were hurrying off to a new restaurant on the Via del' Orso, coming back with notes in my dad's neat handwriting, concise but fractured with exclamation points. *Mullet roe!! lemon peel!!*

• • •

The place was too big.

Even unlocking the back door, you could hear the echo, ashwood floors and newly painted walls resounding with our footsteps.

"I can never find the light switch," said Dad.

Mother turned *hello* into a two-note aria, hoping that Cassandra was down from Tahoe. If Cass had been there that night it might have been different. I might have told the truth, bled words all over the place, got it over with. But with just the three of us, and not even Bernice to cluck over me, we were just people, the way a softball team isn't a team if they happen together by accident.

Bernice—Dad always referred to her as Mrs. Heath—did not actually live here, a fact that relieved my mother, but I think disappointed Dad. He wanted to have a servant, especially one like Bernice, who could manage everything from soufflés to hamburgers. How could you call her a servant, Dad reasoned, if she lived six miles away in Alameda?

Cooking spaghetti is yoga for Dad, necessary for his emotional stability. He took off his bow tie and jacket and tied on an apron. He got a big pot of water simmering, put in a dash of olive oil, while he sipped a short scotch from a cut-glass tumbler Mom gave him for his birthday a couple of years before. He popped the stiff pasta into the water, the spaghetti he buys by the case from a friend with a struggling business in Emeryville.

Several minutes passed without much discussion. I set out some forks and knives and fresh linen napkins. We shared strained small talk, how well the bread had turned out, and whether the heirloom Franciscan wear was still packed in newspaper in the cellar.

Mom never does anything in the kitchen, although tonight she got the lamb out of the fridge and started to put it in the oven. She stopped when Dad made one of his wrinkle-nosed *don't do that*s. She posed here and there in a dressing gown, century-old Japanese silk, stylized birds peering down over her shoulders.

Dad cooked up some of his sauce, six sun-ripened tomatoes whipped to sauce in the blender. He shook the colander, draining the spaghetti, and then we ate.

We only spoke about it later, after supper, our bodies tense with the subject, avoiding it.

"Tell me one thing, since we're talking," said Dad from far away. I was out of his sight, sitting in my favorite chair, a cushioned leather thing in the mostly vacant library. "Jennifer?"

I called that I could barely hear him. Dinner was done, the dishes in the washer, and the lull was over.

He found me. "Come out of here," looking puffy eyed, his fancy clothes replaced by a starched shirt and wool slacks, like someone who intended to sit at a desk all night.

I didn't want this conversation.

"I can't talk to you in here," he said.

Dad had decided on an Asian motif for the living room and had just paid more for a rosewood side table than you'd spend on four years at Yale.

A pile of three-ring notebooks crowded a side table, menus and colorful photographs of food, platters, chafing dishes, tablecloths, a world of bridal cuisine. Now that we had chosen a caterer, Dad kept changing his mind about the linen, the wine, insisting on a frosting expert from New Orleans, "the world's best cake man." Our lives had been an ordeal of more and more arcane decisions, none of the photographers visual enough, none of the florists horticultural enough.

Cass had said if she had to look at another picture of a cake she'd kill herself.

Even now Dad had a wine list in his hand, fake parchment and calligraphy. "Tell me what you were doing," he said, "jogging at night in a deserted place."

"It wasn't night."

"I'm not angry," he said, lifting one hand and letting it fall. When he starts to get mad he backs away from the feeling, like someone stuck with a strange piece of luggage, the kind you aren't supposed to accept at airports. "But you were taking—"

Emotion caught up with him, and he waited for it to pass. "You were taking such a risk."

"I'm sorry," I said, but usually when you say the words some weight is lifted. Nothing lifted, nothing changed. I was afraid he was going to cry.

"I can't think about sauternes at a time like this," he said, flipping the wine list to the carpet. "I'm getting a license for a handgun."

My father can't change a tire. He cuts himself with a can opener. I knew he would shoot his knee off if he bought a gun.

"That would be crazy," I said.

He looked hurt.

"What good would it do me if, if you were sitting at home with a rocket launcher?"

"Plus," he said, "I'm calling Barrow Security."

That had been another concern, who would handle parking and gate crashers at the wedding reception. Barrow was run by former Secret Service agents, I had discovered after a long phone call, and was out of even my dad's league.

"That's overreacting," I said.

"I've been thinking about this," he said. "From now on you'll jog with a bodyguard."

chapter 6

Mom gave me one of her follow-me looks.

Dad nodded that he was through with me and gave me a smile, not one of his publicity-photo half smiles. In those, he's careful not to wrinkle his eyes.

As we left I looked back and he was sitting with his arms on his chair like someone about to be electrocuted, putting up a brave front.

"Don't let Dad buy a gun," I said, following the rustle of her robe down the hall. Only half the paintings were hung on the walls, but all the full-length mirrors were in place, and I had a glimpse of myself, tanned and athletic, good-looking in an ordinary way, nothing like my mother.

"A gun?" she asked, holding the door for me like a hostess.

"And don't let him hire some guys in dark glasses and jogging outfits."

My mother flashes in and out of contact with people. One moment she is caring, full of feeling. And the next she looks around at her surroundings as though she had just materialized from thin air.

"What kind of gun?" she was saying, as though for a moment she saw my dad with a shiny automatic in his hand and liked the image.

"Remember how he shot a staple into his hand?" I said. Two staples, with a staple gun. "And the time he cut a tendon in his finger with his Swiss Army knife?" Blood all over, stitches, tetanus shot.

"I want you to tell me if there's anything I should know," my mother said. She had a cup already waiting for me, a family recipe, intended to make you feel better more from holding it than from sipping the stuff. My cup probably had about ninety percent less booze than Mom's.

We sat in a sort of assistant bedroom, a lieutenant to the main bedroom, which in any case was a showcase room and not where my parents actually slept. For now Mom had given up any resemblance to a fashion model, her eye makeup bruising out down her cheeks and across her temples, her hair claiming a life of its own.

She got out of her chair, kicked it hard into a new position, and sat down like she wanted to be especially mean to the furniture. Sometimes Mom didn't have to fire her secretaries—they quit, worn out by her sudden tempers. Her father had been killed in Laos, during the prequel to Vietnam, blown up by a land mine. I had always wondered if this had given my mother a desire to fight back, get her hands on an enemy. Her sudden moods often gave Dad a headache.

I told her she knew everything.

With my father you get the feeling that some of what you say might show up in his memory of the day's events. With my mother you realize that she'll remember what's best for you, and for her.

After a silence, she said, "I don't care much for that detective. Margate."

Mom hated police. Parking tickets made her seethe. She had witnessed a violent crime when she was a high school student, and she believed police did more harm than good, asking dumb, brutal questions. She had gotten one speeding ticket in her life and she went to traffic court with a lawyer. She won the case.

"I can tell by looking at you this has been a terrible event for you," Mom said. "And I'm not letting that bitch-cop tell me what therapist you're supposed to talk to." Mom uses coarse language way more than Dad, but even so *bitch* sounded especially harsh.

"I want to help the police, if I can." I felt protective toward Detective Margate, doing a tough job, working nights.

My mother looked at me as though she couldn't believe what she was hearing. She lifted her hand like it took a massive effort, so she could finish her drink. I began to wonder how much scotch she had chugged into her cup. "Detective Margate is lying," she said.

I felt a prickling sensation ripple through my nervous system, triggered by the word *lying*. It was like the first time you scuba dive in salt water, straight down, lead weights on your hips, and your mask flash-leaks. You forget the simplest lesson, how to move.

Mom continued, "She says she wants what's best for you."

But you always remember again, after a bad moment. I lifted my eyebrows, a cool, unspoken, "Oh really?"

"The shrink she wants to send you to is Duncan Pierce." Mom used to have an office with a waiting room, a practice, depressives and pill junkies.

I gave a little twitch of my foot: Who's he?

"He's a forensic psychologist," she said. "He's skilled at gathering evidence," she added, "that can be used in a court of law."

It's amazing how long you can sit without moving, a pulse in your wrist, and in a few other body parts, neck, eyelid.

"I'm worried about your state of mind," she said. "You should see a real therapist, not some legal vacuum cleaner."

"I'm okay," I said, sounding pert, like someone saying they didn't want another serving of dessert.

"Police don't think the way we do. If you can help them with their case they'll suck the nerves right out of your body."

"They can't do that," I said with a dry little laugh.

"Yes they can, believe me. What happened tonight?"

"The police were very nice—"

"I mean with the man who attacked you."

"He barely laid a hand on me."

I let this fill the room, Mom waiting to hear more. I could see the unspoken thought in her eyes: Thank heavens this hadn't happened to Cass.

I said, "If there's anything I can do to help catch this man—"

"Before I let a cop psychologist mess with your mind I'll send you to Dr. Yellin." Yellin was the author of about twenty books on recovering from trauma. My mother worshiped him.

"I don't think that will be necessary," I said.

She said, "I'll determine that."

chapter 7

I made the eleven o'clock news. It was a surprise, and I told myself they must have run out of disasters and scandals to report. My attack was right after footage of a four-alarm fire in the financial district.

I hadn't been paying much attention to the TV. My mother kept tapping on my bedroom door, opening it and peering in, cold cream and fatigue giving her a lurid pallor. She asked if I wanted some hibiscus-blossom tea. She wanted to know if I wanted some milk punch, or a nice soak with some of that new bubble bath. Each time I pushed *mute* and said I was fine.

I had met the anchorman at a party in San Francisco, Dave Kiefer, a balding, friendly guy, everybody's uncle. His face usually brightened a little when he read some pleasant news, a poodle stranded in the top of a eucalyptus and rescued by a paramedic. It sombered slightly when he read about a plane crash or ethnic slaughter. His face at the moment was etched with seriousness, making him look old and tired. "Meanwhile, we have a report just coming in on what authorities are saying is another in a series of attacks in the East Bay."

A live report filled the screen, a woman with short black hair and a jacket like Detective Margate's, but better tailored. She stood right in front of the brush beside the path, my path, my blackberry vines, the leaves steel in the TV lights. "Berkeley's Strawberry Canyon was the site of an attempted rape tonight, and authorities suspect that this is another in a series of attacks by the so-called Jogging Rapist."

I sat there on my bed and didn't move, my arms wrapped around my knees.

My bedroom was a vast plateau, posters rolled up, leaning in a distant corner. One of my old favorites was tacked to the wall, *Mustangs, Spirits of the West,* wild horses nuzzling each other, but it was the only horse picture I had bothered to put up. The underwater pictures, parrot fish and bright yellow tangs, were still in their shipping tubes.

The woman reporter referred to me as a sixteen-year-old victim, "in seclusion tonight, with family and friends after a close call, Dave."

I called Marta and asked her if she was watching Channel Five. "God, I always watch Channel Five," she said, her way of telling me she wasn't. Her bedding made gentle thundering noises as she groped around for the remote, and I told her to never mind.

"I always watch the same news, or at least I have it on," said Marta. Her actual name is Martina, but no one calls her that. "I watch it all the time. I found it. It's an ad."

"Turn it off."

"I think the batteries are about dead in my remote," said Marta. "I'm shaking it and it still doesn't work the way it's supposed to."

Cassandra just about destroyed my friendship with Marta by pointing out that Marta wasn't very bright. I was furious, and hurt. Cass pointed out that Marta repeats the same statement four or five times, using slightly different words, bulking out her conversation so that she seems to be saying more than she is.

It was just like Cass to needle me about a friend, but then I started to listen to Marta, and it was true. Cass is often cruel, and right. Talking with Marta drove me crazy for a while, until we both took scuba lessons together and her mom started taking us to their bungalow on Monterey Bay on weekends. There aren't very many rules that can save your life, and one of them is: Dive with a buddy. Marta is one of those people you want to have around.

I told her what had just been on the news, and added, "That was me."

For a while there wasn't anything coming out of the telephone but things like "Oh, Jennifer" and "My God, Jennifer, are you all right?" meaning what we had all come to mean by *all right.*

"It's hell around here," I said.

"Is your dad going crazy?"

I knew what she meant, and in his own way my father was going through tremendous turmoil. But Marta's father is artistic director for the East Bay Theater, a foul-mouthed, hotheaded guy who had suffered three heart attacks and now lived on Paxil and took long vacations at their place on Monterey Bay. When he was upset, people knew it down the block. I had heard Marta say that it was a good thing her dad was a pacifist or he would have killed someone.

I said that my dad didn't go crazy; he suffered. My father admired Marta's parents and said the Emmits were "rarer than radium," which is Dad-talk for really special. Mr. Emmit thought Dad was brilliant, buying every kind of mustard my dad recommended, even the yellow Chinese powder that tastes like ant poison. My mom thought it was a shame Mrs. Emmit couldn't lose the weight, but Lynn Emmit was perhaps my mother's closest friend.

"How's your mom behaving?" Marta asked.

I told her that Mother would have been a better detective than any of the cops.

"Are you sure you're okay?" Marta had been the first to notice that my face had taken on a gaunt, sleep-hungry look in recent weeks. Months of bad sleep were catching up with me.

I assured her that I would survive.

"You need some downtime," said Marta.

That's what scuba people call time spent on the sea floor.

I did take a bath, and soaked in a slurry of salts and essential oils of valerian and poppy.

Back in my half-acre room I toyed with the tape recorder Dad had given me as a stocking stuffer the Christmas before, "Just like mine." It was top-of-the line, voice activated. Dad had given up on taking notes, and you could hear him at six in the morning, downstairs on the running machine, panting, "Cut fresh dough into half-inch squares."

When I spoke, "Testing one, two," the red record light came on, stayed on a few moments, and then went out because I wasn't saying anything.

chapter 8

I got up early, after watching the Discovery Channel until three in the morning, sleepless as usual. You can watch the bower bird knit his wedding decor from parrot feathers and monkey hair, but the documentaries hurry on to the meatier footage we are all supposed to prefer, cheetahs getting full extension, zero to sixty in no time at all, zebras zigzagging all over the veldt.

You wonder what the wildebeest thinks, a family of leopards chewing on her hindquarters, the grazing creature looking around panting, nowhere to go, still very much alive.

Sometimes I start to watch what is happening in the distance, if a documentary or the plot of a movie is too violent. Off at the edge of the screen there is usually a tree full of long-necked cranes, or a blurry, bovine shape just standing there. In the goriest gangster movie, in the forefront you might see extras ducking for cover in their thirties overcoats, but at the same time, beyond everything, a finch that doesn't belong in the movie, or real wind fluttering a leaf.

I had slept a couple of hours, the cheap sleep you get on an airliner, my mouth hanging open, head full of thoughts. My hand was stiff and sore. I laced on my running shoes, the left one stained with a kiss of blackberry. It would not smear, and spit wouldn't make it rub off.

My left foot tends to overpronate, rolling in too much with every step. It isn't a serious problem except that my left shoe starts to lean in a little when it's flat on the floor. I burn through shoes, and I try all the brands, every major company. I wear a dual-density midsole in my left shoe, taking it to a sport-tech store to be redesigned before I do any serious running.

I wrap white adhesive tape around the aglets, the plastic tip of the shoelaces. Otherwise the aglet often splits after about a week of nipping the street. The laces get that frayed look, which I hate. Miss Friday, the track coach at Lloyd-Fairhill School, says the thicker the sole the more likely you are to develop tendon trouble, especially shinsplints. I suspect Friday is one of those coaches who would like to see athletes run marathons barefooted.

Predawn hush greeted me, five A.M., a few neighbors out jogging with their dogs and hefty neighbors running off those calories from fat. This is a safe place to run, and I make it even more safe by keeping to the streets with plenty of light and doing most of my miles at the junior high quarter-mile loop about a mile away, a nice crushed brick track that glows in the rising dawn.

I kept stopping to look back, car-poolers picking up passengers with briefcases, ready for the long drive to Silicon Valley. The sky was the color of dark steel, and sometimes this early you can look at things more easily than you can at full noon; there is less glare. But there were more shadows down each street than I had ever noticed before, more dark, lightless shafts behind the sycamores. What could have been a commuter wiping the dew off his sports car looked like a figure crouching at the starting blocks, getting set to race after me.

Dad had his postworkout glow, after three miles on his machine in the exercise room. He had a white towel around his neck and wore one of his old, premegabucks sweatsuits, baggy gray cotton.

He snapped his cell phone shut and tossed it onto the coffee table. "I'm furious," he said. He sounded calm, but I knew better. "I finally got hold of Cassandra."

"How is she?" I asked, dropping into the sectional sofa, fat white pillows with an ivory pattern, duck bills, or—once you were informed—lotus leaves.

"She's pissed I woke her up. She says she is sorry to hear about your 'incident,' and she's coming home tonight about ten, as planned."

"There's nothing she can do," I said. It was fine with me if I put off seeing Cass until the wedding.

I knew that Cass and Danny, her fiancé, were sharing our cabin, romping all over the master bedroom. Danny was supposed to be in San Diego, playing golf with his dad, a retired VIP with the state department. Cass was supposed to be working on her tan with a couple of girlfriends. My parents would not have died if they knew the truth, but this pretense spared everyone having to think about Danny and Cass giving the heirloom bird's-eye maple bed a workout.

"We have to change the flowers," he said. "I woke up last night with the realization that yellow roses are all wrong."

"Roses," I said, one of Mom's techniques, repeating a key word and letting the client vent. There was something Cass had told me about Dad, but I didn't know how to begin to ask.

"Dr. Theobald has beautiful white hair. We need blue-white hybrid roses to match his coloring." Dr. Theobald—pronounced *Tibuld*—is a Unitarian minister, about ninety years old, who met my father at one of the Season of Hope fund-raisers. My father is about as religious as a doorstop, but when he learned that the old gentleman was dean of the Unitarian seminary in Berkeley, my parents had begun inviting the him to the occasional party. The clergyman turned out to be a real gem, with a voice like a wildlife movie narrator. If he said, "This chardonnay is delicious," it was like the earth itself had opened up and complimented the hostess.

"That's dozens of long-stemmed roses," I said, "for those wicker thingies—"

"So why not get on the phone to the florist and tell him I want the Jessica Friedlander Brodie hybrid or the April Thursday long-stems. And there's a couple other of ideas on my tape recorder. I have to be in L.A. all day, wringing someone's neck."

"Whose?"

"They're planning to give the set for my show the 'trattoria look.' Chianti in straw, and hanging Italian sausages, and maybe some fake plastic grapes." It was only a series of pilots, sample shows. Cass and I half hoped no network would actually buy the series. Dad was getting up too many nights, eating sourdough and Stilton, almond butter and water crackers, lasagna, leg of lamb—whatever he could get his hands on.

"Whose neck?"

"What happens when I do sushi?" he said, ignoring my question. "Or when I talk about the First Thanksgiving, with Little Sicily all over the place? I don't want you to go running until the sun comes up."

"It *is* up."

"Run on the machine, that's what it's for. How are you feeling?"

I said I felt good.

"Look at that printout I got off the Web," he said. "That stuff's supposed to be better than Mace."

A page on the rosewood coffee table depicted a spray can with arms and legs. It was standing triumphant, biceps bulging, over a prone male body. *Karate in a Can.*

"You wear it clipped to your shirt. Someone messes with you, you knock him flat."

"Maybe you should just buy me a shotgun," I said.

Dad gave me the look he uses on headwaiters who say the table isn't quite ready.

Dad had to take a twelve-gauge out of the hands of a liquor-wired neighbor a couple of years before, a pensioned freeway construction exec with bladder cancer. The chief of police wrote him a letter saying Dad was the "kind of citizen Oakland needs." For months afterward the pop of a motor scooter made Dad go white.

I had forgotten, or maybe remembered without knowing it. Dad had even taken the novel *Shogun* to Goodwill because it reminded him of the Remington pump-action our fellow citizen had leveled at Dad's face.

"Come with me," he said. "Fly down to L.A. for the day. You can meet my producer."

"What's he like?" I asked, choosing my words carefully.

"'What's he like,'" he echoed, with a chuckle. "*She's* very knowledgeable." Dad respected knowledge, believed in it.

"Really." This was more Cass's intonation than Mom's, icy charm, keep away from children and pets.

"You could load those files into my laptop for me on the plane, sit by the pool, run spell-check though my notes."

I had to feel a little compassion for my father. Dad moved the knockout spray ad to a safe place, under a century-old crystal ashtray. We used it as a paperweight; both my dad's parents have emphysema. He thought I was going to spend the day in L.A. watching him tell people maybe the Italian restaurant look was a good idea after all.

Doors slammed in far away places, Dad getting ready for the airport.

chapter 9

Bernice is a tall, correct woman with black hair, a touch of gray at the temples. Dad said she had a "troubled personal history." She was of Dad's many projects, people he knows and helps. We had not met her at all until several weeks ago, but she knew from the start that I couldn't stand the wrinkly skin that forms on hot chocolate. At first Mom would have rather let some of the rooms remain dusty than have this female general marching up and down the stairs. But something about Bernice pleased even my mother. Bernice seemed to have known us for years.

Her name was pronounced in a slightly unusual way: *Burn-us,* with the accent on the first syllable, not *Burr-niece.* The only person who always won a smile from Bernice was me, and it was a little embarrassing how much she clammed up around Cassandra. I was very self-conscious about seeing Bernice this morning, sure that my parents had filled her in on the Incident. So I was surprised when I slipped into the kitchen and got her usual "good morning," smile, no extra concern.

She makes wonderful bread, pouring ingredients into the bread machine, wheat germ, handfuls of oats, sage honey, bran, never measuring. And out of the machine come loaves of heaven. I had a slice of her toast, with the smallest possible touch of her apricot preserves, taking my time, not wanting to tell her.

Mom came down from the bedroom, dressed for work, a boardroom pinstripe and a strawberry sherbet scarf. She said, "Bernice, I need a word with you."

Bernice returned pale and drawn, taller than ever.

She looked away from me, sifting flour, like I wasn't there, as Mom bustled in, poured herself a tidy half cup of coffee, added some nonfat milk, and drank it off, all without a change of expression. My mother looked years older this morning, her hair just about recovered, her eye makeup perfect, if you like that sort of thing. She couldn't hide the parentheses around her mouth, the fine wrinkles, or the waves of weary tension that flowed out of her like cold weather.

Mom gave me an embrace, dangerously close to damaging her makeup. "I'll call you from the office. Put that new little phone in your backpack. And turn the ringer on, so you can hear it."

In the morning light there was no talk of me seeing a psychiatrist, as there had been no mention of bodyguards.

Then I was alone with Bernice.

Bernice was not acting the way I expected. I had imagined a hug of concern, a promise of tiramisu or crème caramel, and a long talk about capital punishment, which she believed was the foundation of a sane society.

I didn't expect this silence.

"It's a sickening thing," she said after a very long time.

"Bernice, I'm all right."

"You think you are."

"Nothing much happened—he just barely touched me."

Bernice was sifting way more flour than she needed, soft billows of unbleached white drifting across the marble pastry slab.

I made a shrug, which was wasted; she wasn't looking. My shoulder was stiff.

After a silence she said, "Jennifer, this will haunt you."

Detective Margate called just after nine.

She said that she needed to talk. The sounds of the police station were audible in the background, phones trilling, muted voices. She had left her office door open, maybe to give me the full effect. "As soon as it's convenient," she said.

I said that I would be happy to help.

chapter 10

It was an unmarked car, coffee-ice-cream brown, a whiplash antenna above the gas cap.

Detective Ronert sat in the back seat, busy with a ballpoint pen and a clipboard. He said good morning and asked me how I was doing.

I told him I was okay, and he looked at me searchingly, as though he hoped this was true. I kept looking back at him, asking him about the paperwork he had to do, even though it gave me a crick in my neck. He explained that detecting crime was all record keeping. "If we draw our weapons we have to account for each shot."

"What happens if there's a shoot-out?" I asked.

He said, "We have to draw a yellow circle around every little hole."

"Seat belt," said Detective Margate.

I worked at getting the buckle to fasten, and at last Margate had to reach over and do it for me, smelling faintly of soap.

She drove about fifteen miles an hour, eyeing a dog-minder across the street, a muscular man walking four dogs at once, the little dust mop planting a turd in the gutter. Our new neighborhood was replete with child-care experts pushing strollers jammed with four toddlers at once, not to mention the corps of tree surgeons and gardeners who started bright and early, nipping and tucking.

Detective Margate took a great deal of interest in the way the dog-man pulled on an oversize plastic glove and knelt, gathering the poop into a Baggie.

"I guess he likes animals," I said.

"Or else he really needs a job." Detective Margate sped up. "It reminds me of what *we* do," she said.

I thought that she meant all of us living creatures, excreting solid waste.

"Police, I mean," she said. "Detectives."

"Ask her about the drag and drop," said Ronert.

"We need to find out how far the attacker dragged you," she said. "And where he let you go."

"He didn't drag me anywhere."

"Not even a couple of meters?" she asked.

Meters, I noted, not yards. I told her I didn't think so.

"The FBI might still be interested," said Ronert from the back seat. "If it's anything like attempted kidnapping."

"Kidnapping," said Detective Margate, with gently mocking good humor. "Detective Ronert toured the FBI when he was a kid."

"It's only a little farther," I cautioned her, as the detective whisked through an intersection.

She pulled over to the curb under a eucalyptus that was tagged with a bright green sticker. The roots had buckled the sidewalk, sections of concrete sticking up like playing cards. Someone had probably stumbled and sued the city. The tree was marked for destruction.

"When you were jogging last evening," the detective began. "Before the attack—" She set the parking brake and eased the gears into neutral. I had done well in driver's education, but my favorite part of any driving experience was turning off the ignition and getting out of the car. Dad said I'd get a Fiat when I graduated.

"I was running," I corrected her. I run or I walk; jogging is for people who lack determination.

"When you were running you might have seen a car parked, up by the botanical gardens."

"Maybe," I said, meaning: maybe not.

"Because the perp must have driven up the canyon and pulled off the road."

"Okay," I said, meaning: I'm listening.

"It's all no parking. Unless you saw a car with its hazard lights on, someone with a flat tire or a stall."

"I didn't."

"You sound sure," said the voice from the back seat.

I craned my neck to look at Detective Ronert, his sympathetic face stuck in the farthest possible corner of the back.

I said, "I can't remember a particular vehicle."

"That late in the day all the botanical garden staff is gone," she said. "So any car in the parking lot—" She glanced into her side mirror, and a bicyclist flashed by, pumping hard down College Avenue.

"So," she continued, after watching the cyclist's butt disappear down the street. "Were there any cars parked there?"

"There could have been," I said.

"But you can't remember?" she asked.

I made an I'm-trying frown.

"Because failure to recall the run-up to a crime is very common, and these back-canceled impressions are what we need to uncover."

What *would* I have been able to recall, I asked myself.

"The point is—we have some tire tread," the detective was saying. "There was a car that parked just beyond the gardens, up behind a pine tree, like someone trying to hide. If you saw a vehicle secluded during your run—"

"You can match the tread to the car," I prompted, like the smartest kid in class.

"We did already, it was a Volvo, not new. They're very easy to identify, all those European tires. But the car could have parked there any time within the last couple of days. We can't search for all the ten-year old Volvos."

"Ten-year-old tires would be pretty worn out."

"They were."

I made myself look like someone searching her memory. Then I offered a helpless smile.

"All the other attacks have been in more urban areas. San Jose State University, the Hayward BART station, the old Montgomery Ward building." She left some silence between statements, like someone who never had to rush. "How far up the canyon did you jog, Jennifer?"

"All the way up to the Lawrence Hall of Science." This was untrue, but my voice betrayed nothing. Besides, I could run tougher hills than that.

"So you passed that funny-looking pine tree, with the twisted branches."

"I can't remember a particular tree." But then, like a poker player turning over a card, I saw it clearly in my mind, the tree she was talking about. I had seen it as I surveyed the canyon in recent weeks, a stunted Monterey pine. "The one like this, arms all over the place."

Detective Margate made a smile by pressing her lips together. "We can forget about the Volvo, right?"

I made the kind of exaggerated sigh Dad gives when Cass drives him crazy.

Detective Margate took her time, shifting into drive, releasing the parking brake. "We need you to help us, Jennifer. And we need your parents to consent."

"I'd love to help. The trouble is, Mom hates police shrinks."

The car accelerated, and we began passing cars in the slow lane. "I was in Strawberry Canyon until well after midnight last night and studied that path up and down the slope. I just don't see our perpetrator hiding in the poison oak."

"You're going to send me to a doctor who'll get me to remember." I watched the store fronts drift by.

"It'll help us immeasurably," she said.

"He'll stick a needle into me."

"That's not how Dr. Pierce works," she said, in a tone of great kindness, like the world's best nurse. "He uses memory regression. The other victims have cooperated. If nothing else works, he uses hypnosis."

I stared at her profile.

She asked, "Where do you work?"

chapter

11

At first Animal Heaven looks like just another pet store, cheese-flavored chew toys for the family Rottweiler dangling next to a display of choke collars.

Mr. DaGama, the owner, spoke English with a Cuban accent and could soothe even the most high-strung whippet with a touch. Marta had found me the job, three or four half days a week during the summer, tending the boarded animals in the back room.

The aviaries behind the main shop were a wonderful secret, zebra finches, lovebirds, conures, cockatiels, parakeets, and at one end of the room the royalty of the kingdom, macaws and cockatoos, all of them prized by their traveling owners and left with us because the animals thrived here.

Cass says "Animal Heaven" sounds like a pet cemetery. Cass used to skip up and down the sidewalk, killing ants.

Dad always said we traveled too much to take care of a dog, and Mom said cats could not be trusted.

I loved the pet store. Droopy, eighty-year-old Amazons perked up under our heat lamps, and egg-bound canary hens laid their eggs after all, singing their happily tuneless female-finch song.

I slung my leather purse/backpack into a corner. I felt light-headed, and colors were garish, the display of dog dishes, unbreakable, gleaming, primary colors, made me feel like throwing up.

Mr. DaGama followed me into the back room, a newspaper folded in his hand. "You're okay," he said, a tone of surprise.

Marta, or Marta's mom, must have called him. I asked how Byron was doing.

"Byron lives," he said. Sometimes he ladled out his accent, not trying to speak normal English. *Bee-roan leaves.* He shook open the *Tribune. Suspect New Attack in Serial Terror.* I sat down on a big paper bag of sunflower seeds as I scanned the column for my name. I couldn't find it.

"Marta's coming in soon," said Mr. DaGama.

"The African gray is saying something," I said, to change the subject.

The gray parrot hadn't been a talker when his new owners left him here five days before, heading for a camping trip, hiking Molokai to the historical leper colony. The new parrot words did not sound like much, but they had the shape and intonation of human speech.

"Jennifer," Mr. DaGama was saying, "this country is too gentle with wicked people." The way he said my name made it sound exotic, the *J* given just a curl of his tongue. "A man like this should be horsewhipped in the town square."

A headache started up, a thrum as steady and ugly as a motor inside my brain. "I can take care of myself." This was new for me, a flickering aluminum flame at the edge of my vision.

"I bet you anything this criminal just got out of prison. I expect he is at liberty not one or two weeks. And he begins his old ways."

"No harm was done," I said. Something about Mr. DaGama's careful, correct English made me speak similar sentences.

"Jennifer, I think that harm was done," he said.

Byron was a sulfur-crested cockatoo with the chalky, gnarled beak of a very old bird. He sat in his food dish, and as I approached, the crest fanned upward on his head, erect in greeting. Byron's owner was a professor, away in England lecturing on how planets are born. Byron had started sneezing late last week, bubbles of snot crusting his nostrils, and, as I watched, Mr. DaGama put a heavy dose of avian antibiotic into his water dish.

Marta flings herself into a room, but she never knocks so much as a chew toy off the display table, or slips on a wet floor.

Mr. DaGama was cleaning up after an elderly teacup pug had peed a tiny bit, excited at his new rubber chew-bone, "flavored with real beef." Marta hurried into the back room. If she had theme music it would be drums and cymbals.

"I called Quinn," said Marta, first thing, before she bothered with "good morning."

This startled me. "You didn't."

"I called him and talked to his dad, and then I talked to him in person." Marta is mouse-blond, but the sun bleaches her gold. Like me, she's got shoulders and hips, and she stands about my height. In volleyball, she can spike the ball better than anyone, but my serves drop in.

I thought of crashing the parakeet cage over her head, but parakeets can be startled to death very easily. Quinn had moved to Reno with his family, and I had almost completely trained myself not to think about him.

"I knew you'd want him to know," she said. "That you'd want him to hear the news, but that you couldn't, probably, bring yourself to tell him yourself."

Usually when people talk about what you would have wanted, you're a corpse and unable to overhear. My dad has headaches like this, migraines that send him to the medicine cabinet. I had never experienced anything like it.

"Quinn was very upset," Marta was saying. She reached into a conure's cage and looped a squabbling, half-wild bird onto her finger. The scarlet and azure bird had bit everyone, even Mr. DaGama, until this moment. "Quinn was really worried about it and wanted to know how you were doing. He thought you'd be in a hospital, and I said you were at home."

Marta drove me home in her Toyota, a car with stuffing bursting out of the upholstery. Marta was definite that she wanted to be a veterinarian, but with a specialty in either tropical fish or birds of the rain forest. She was fascinated by any living creature with symptoms of illness, got wide-eyed with concern, and needed a running account on any symptom. Including me.

"You don't have any diarrhea, though," said Marta. "Do you? Loose stools are a key in diagnosing illness. In any animal. And that includes humans."

Sometimes when Marta starts to talk she never stops. I said, "Stop the car."

But diving or driving, Marta is deft. She had the car at the curb in a wink, and I opened the passenger door and deposited the contents of my stomach into the gutter.

Bernice has a brace of corporals and sergeants. They creep, snipping the privet bush in the garden, dusting the bottom rungs of the dining room chairs. A dust expert knelt on the stairs, spraying a substance onto his yellow cloth, applying it to the bare wood on either side of the Turkish carpet.

Slung low to the ground, feeling like a rhino, I stumbled past this dust engineer. I found myself in Dad's bathroom looking hard into my reflection, brown hair, brown eyes. I don't use a conditioner on my hair, just baby shampoo, brush it. When Cass is around sometimes she braids it for me.

Dad's new medicine cabinet was replete with Demerol and Tylenol with codeine. He had Percodan, generic oxycodone, and painkiller suppositories, in case he became too nauseated to swallow. But he hoards old pills, in case he needs them. The capsules outlast their sell-by dates, some of the prescription labels still sporting Dr. Rigby's name, an internist who retired a year ago.

. . .

I slept, huddled in my bed in my shadowy cavern, and as I drowsed I heard voices. I sat up at one point, sure that I heard Detective Margate downstairs. I strained my ears, but then I decided the muffled voice belonged to Mom.

Footsteps tiptoed up the stairs. Someone knocked softly and peeked in.

It was Bernice. She gave me a cool, wet washcloth, like a Victorian remedy for the vapors.

"Let yourself rest," said Bernice. Life for someone like Bernice is a matter of allowing—letting herself sit, permitting herself a moment of rest on the back step in the afternoon sun.

When I woke the headache was gone, and I felt that strange, deceitful sensation of lying down on a nice day, sunlight slicing through the crack in the curtains. I heard Dad's voice somewhere far away, and I knew this was impossible—he was in L.A.

I lay still, looking at the empty landscape of my ceiling, but the rich drowsiness was over. I put my feet on the floor and sat, doing a systems check, shoulder, blackberry scratches, bruised hand. I experimented mentally with a prepared statement, sounding like something Mr. DaGama would say: *None of it is true.*

Dad makes the gentlest noise when he knocks on my door, an excuse-me-for-living tip-tap.

I felt a ripple of guilt as he peeked in.

I said, "You're supposed to be gone."

"I told them I'd come down in a day or two."

He sat on the end of the bed, the mattress canting subtly with his weight.

"I think it must be in the chromosomes," I said. I felt a little wobbly. I had taken two very large capsules, choked down with not enough water. Once I had heard Dad reading the warning leaflets that came with the pills, possible seizure and coma if you overdosed.

He made the pleasant expression he wears when he doesn't get what I'm saying.

"I inherited your headaches," I said.

I didn't mean this reproachfully, but Dad put a hand to his head.

"My mother had them, too," he said. "About one Sunday a month she couldn't get out of bed."

"I thought she never got sick." It was a family legend, Grandma's iron constitution, until she smoked so many Kools they had to hook her to an oxygen tank.

I thought, I'd rather get double pneumonia than another migraine.

"You'll never guess what I have for you," he said.

chapter

12

The dashboard clock said 4:36.

Summer afternoon, plenty of sunlight, lawn sprinklers chattering, a breath of spray across the windshield. If you rarely swallow painkillers you know why they call them *drugs*. I felt about three pages behind everything that happened, the sun too bright.

"I told you keep your eyes shut."

I shut them an exaggerated way, bunched up my face, and then feathered one eye open just a bit.

"Shut tight," he said.

Dad was prime at times like this, in control. I've seen him sweep into his restaurant five minutes before opening, the regular chef out with the flu, the staff rattled, all elbows and feet. One of Dad's pep talks and the evening is won.

I used to want to be a chef, soups my specialty, the kind

you make from a simmered
Then I wanted to be an arcl
My test scores are a range o
below average at telling w
hole. Mom said it was hard
never fought to change any

It wasn't a long drive, bi
cresting, my stomach feeling
scent.

You can tell when you're
eucalyptus. The air smells clean, like mothballs and fresh,
spice countryside. The tires crunched and whispered up a
dirt road, shadows playing across my eyelids. Jays called,
smart birds who know exactly what a car is and probably
count the passengers.

I caught a whiff of manure, a golden, sun-ripened scent,
and the hollow wooden buildings echoing the breathy
thrum of Dad's car as he eased it along, the independent
suspension handling the heavy ruts.

I told myself, surely not.

It was just my imagination.

"Still shut?" Dad was saying.

I gave a tentative laugh, knowing my face was comical,
squinched up, but committed to the rules.

My vision was having trouble adjusting to the patches
of black shadow, scissor-bright sun, light reflecting off a
water trough and the arcing blades of eucalyptus leaves.

I knew Sandalwood Ranch well, only a mile and a half
from our new house, but another world. I was delaying,
blinking, pretending, letting my sight settle on the comfy,

boxy black interi
white muzzled
The hors
loft and
Sh
b

down

r of a stable, two horses gazing out,
pintos who had nothing to do with me.
Dad was indicating was dancing sideways, all
spirit, at the limit of a long, looping bridle.
was wheat yellow, with a blond mane, her nostrils
unette. When a fly touched withers her skin jumped,
shaking off the insect with a lightning shiver. Her head
tossed, but her eyes were calm, taking in her wrangler, the
gleaming rails of the corral, everything but us.

Even with the words spoken, I was sure I had misunderstood.

My dad took in my silence and stepped toward the corral, propping one leg up on the wooden rail.

"Flower's all excited, Mr. Thayer," said Tommy Dixon, dressed like a cowboy, with his hand on the end of the leather restraint, wheeling and following the mare's ballet, his face in a silent laugh.

"Bring her over, Tommy," said my dad.

The horse dipped her head, nostrils flaring, her breath blowing a eucalyptus leaf out of her path. She gave a few sweeping nods, the kind horses make when they are alive to what is on the ground, maybe starting to feel hungry, but aware of other creatures, too, horses nickering, people standing, a man with his hand outstretched.

Dad reached out and nearly touched her, the horse keen at the sight of his hand, thrusting her muzzle toward his face, but holding back. Then my father withdrew his touch, and turned to me.

He said it again. "She's yours."

And this time I couldn't pretend not to hear, as I

watched my hand rise and almost touch the soft, silken wrinkles of her mouth. I knew how she would feel before I laid a hand on her, although I had ridden only a few horses in my life, as a thirteen-year-old, when Marta and I took lessons.

I touched her warm breath—hot, really, too moist to be exhalation from an animal's lungs. Then she offered her muzzle to me and jerked away after a kiss, my hand, her lower jaw. And then back again, allowing me to stroke her, thrusting her head between my father's chuckle and my silence.

Dad let the car roll slowly up the hard-packed dirt road, the sun brilliant beyond the bay.

"Desert Flower," he said. "Pretty name. I made some phone calls to some of my contacts in the horse world. Tommy Dixon said this is the first time an animal like this has been on the market in a couple of years."

"She isn't actually a *race* horse," I said.

"Just a horse with an interesting ancestry," he said. "Distant relation to a horse who used to race in England, Desert Orchid."

We were home before either of us spoke again, the black iron gate swinging open. Then he said, "Tommy'll take care of the horse, him and his staff. Those guys are very knowledgeable."

I'd need to ride it every day, I told myself, and concern myself with its psychological and physical demands.

I had outgrown horses, moved on in my mental life, and was now more interested in sea otters and tropical birds.

Dad was remembering a former version of me, trying to give an earlier image of me something we never could have afforded in the old days.

My dad swerved around the red, four-wheel drive Jeep in the driveway, giving the vehicle a long look, maybe wondering if he should have picked something sportier for the family car.

"Great moments in science," he said, mock-TV-announcer. "Cass is here early."

I wondered how long I could hide in the car.

chapter

13

You hear about the aftermath of a migraine, a feeling of tranquillity. I felt tired and apprehensive. A soreness in my shoulder throbbed, a neon nerve, flashing on and off. I knew what people would think of me if they knew the truth, and they would be right.

There's something about Cass that draws you forward. You want to see what mood she's in, what she has to say. You can't stay away.

Although you can delay for a while. The back garden was a hodgepodge, tall straight junipers and closely trimmed hedges, a maze that didn't lead anywhere. A knot garden, interlocking sage and lavender bushes, attracted orange skipper moths and work-dazed honeybees. The shadows fell across the patio from the massive square-topped yew.

The previous owner had been an economics professor turned state senator, a man who had finally drifted off to

Arizona, delighted to see "a thriving bunch" taking the big garden off his hands. As a little girl I would have lost myself in the secret harbors of nasturtium and rosemary. Even now I was tempted to slip among the climbing roses, dodge a few late-hour wasps, and make a point of staying away from Cassandra.

The wasps troubled Dad. He'd have a cup of coffee in his hand and pull a bench out under the wisteria, and one of those little yellow bullets would have him hunching his shoulders and saying, "I'm all right, they don't really bother me." As a little boy, the story went, he had nearly swallowed a dead wasp in his lemonade.

Cass had already fixed me on her radar. There was no clear evidence for this, but I knew.

So I walked right up to her. She stood in that distinctive way she has, absent-mindedly rubbing one shin with the other. She has a natural physical glow, effortlessly good at tennis, arm wrestling, arguing. If you walked down the street with Cass, she was the one people turned to watch. She was standing on the patio, among pots of leafy bamboo and dwarf pines still wearing their plastic nursery tabs, instructions on light and water.

Cass was flipping the pages of a garden magazine, spotting Post-its Dad had inserted to mark an especially pleasant floral arrangement. But you could tell she was just being polite to Dad. All the red-letter decisions had been made, and I suspected Cass was just looking for a splendid two-page spread of yellow roses, to prove to Dad that if they had to make a change it should be a clergyman who got axed, not flowers.

She heard me coming and saw me out of the corner of

her eye, all the way, so she had to whisk through the last few pages of the magazine before she could fling it down and give me a big hug, sisterly and strong, saying how glad she was to see me all in one piece.

She said it like a joke, something casual and barely meant, but she took me by the chin, the way an adult will take a very young child, and looked right into my eyes.

"Where are you hurt?" she asked.

I indicated with gestures, the way a stewardess gives the preflight instructions, exit rows, oxygen masks, accompanying the voice on the intercom.

But there wasn't any commentary, just my silence.

Cassandra shook her head solemnly. Cass is twenty-one and blitzed through high school with sterling grades, with a little coercion of the teachers from Mom. Cass tore through her undergraduate years with honors in everything, and was all set to continue graduate school at Stanford, studying sports psychology.

Mom had argued that the field was beneath her intellectual level, but because Danny Powell was planning to go into orthopedic medicine, with a special emphasis on the knee, this was just another chapter in the continuing story of Cass, where nothing went wrong. Danny's father owned a house near Holland Park in London, and acreage in Sonoma County.

Cass's hair was curly, hay blond, and although she wore it long she never needed a perm. She was prettier in photos than she was in real life, but she had always had male companions, tennis partners and Ping-Pong rivals and, I knew by my own private mental seismograph, intimate male friends since the day after Thanksgiving of her sixteenth year. Her boyfriends had always been the sons of corporate lawyers or vascular surgeons, young men my mother had been pleased to ask over for dinner.

Mom doesn't flutter, but she does take up alternating positions, from corner to corner, seeking attention, and occasionally giving it. Dad couldn't help beaming at us, pleased to see his family together for a few minutes beside the miniature lemon tree. Other dads would have used the opportunity for a few Polaroids, everyone showing their grins. Dad has a good memory, so he wandered around with his hands in his pockets, shooting us glances with a smile, storing up his visual impressions of the evening.

There was the obligatory question from Dad, "Hear from Danny?" As if we all didn't assume she had dropped him off in Larkspur before lucking out with the traffic all the way here.

"Danny says hi," she said.

Even Mom smiled, and you could see the shadows lift from her face. I had to laugh a little, too, along with Cass, because we were pleased to have dispatched with Danny in such a small number of words. Danny was an accomplishment as much as a person, a victory Cass had won that no longer needed to be discussed.

Supper was chilled smoked sea bass and a pasta salad, followed by a lime sorbet so tart it brightened all our eyes. Some evenings Bernice worked late, attending us like an old family retainer, not someone who had worked for Dad five and a half weeks. This was one of her nights to observe the family, making sure we used our fish forks.

What Bernice was really waiting for, I suspect, was a good word from Cassandra. Cass rarely ate here—she lived across the bay in an apartment in Palo Alto. But the few times Cass had complimented Bernice on her scones or offered a suggestion about serving filtered water, not water from the tap, you could see the strain on both of them.

"This is just marvelous," Cass said, as Bernice stepped into the room to survey her dominion.

"Thank you, Miss Thayer," said Bernice.

Dad raised an eyebrow.

I was privately relieved when Dad said he'd "take coffee" in the library, unpacking a shipment of new books. I knew he was hoping some of us would join him, but Mom said she had to make some phone calls, and I filtered out through the walls, like smoke, or tried to.

But Cass made some sort of artful exit a minute or two later and followed me into the dark garden, an interplay of lights from upstairs windows, shadowy night between the hedges.

I sensed her mental weapons-system lock on to me. She paused. She made a visual confirmation of my whereabouts, and then she took a long way around, under the wisteria beneath my parents' bedroom.

"So tell me what happened, Jenny," said Cass.

Cass often started her chats this way. The *so* always irritates me, brushing aside anything you might have been thinking or about to say.

Her request was hardly a surprise, but I could not speak before she added, "I heard about Desert What's-its-name."

"She'll need a firm hand," I said.

One of Cass's artful pauses followed, and then, "Tell me what happened."

"I've told everyone so much," I said.

"It sounds like you have," said Cassandra.

"I was very fortunate," I said, keeping my tone neutral.

Cass tilted her head to one side, showing off her sixth sense, hearing what I was not saying. Cass was always getting jewelry for her birthday, even as a child, an heirloom opal bracelet, an amethyst brooch, astonishing gifts Mom planned months ahead. I was the one who always tore off the gift wrap to yet another book—full-color photos of bears in their mountain kingdoms, eagles in their last refuge.

"Can I tell you what I'm afraid is happening, Jennifer?" she said at last.

I gave a shrug: Tell me if you want.

"Forgive me for what I'm going to say, Jenny, but I am afraid that you might have gone up to Strawberry Canyon with the idea of pretending." She said *pretending* like it was a despicable word, foreign, and pronounceable only by the carefully educated.

When I did not respond, she continued, "You might have made believe that an assault took place. You were always the one making your dolls have adventures, getting kidnapped or—"

"Why would I do that?" I asked.

Cassandra understands the importance of timing.

"Maybe you thought," she said, "enough attention was being paid to me, it's your turn."

"I don't think you're being fair."

Amazingly, I was able to say this without sounding like the proverbial little sister, a quaver in my voice. Cass had always been the one adults spoke to, engaging her in conversation as an equal, her poise deceiving them. They told her all about the bond market, their favorite movies, where to buy the best Italian wines. She asked all the right questions, *Oh, really?* Only I could see the flat indifference in Cass, how little she cared.

Cass didn't mention her talk with me a few nights ago. I had expressed doubts about my maid-of-honor-dress, and hinted that maybe one of her Stanford psych major friends would do the job more elegantly. Cass does not *get* angry. She exposes the anger that is always there, ready.

"Why would I do such a thing?" I heard myself ask—a blunder, I knew as soon as I said it.

"Think of the power," she said. "Think of the position of strength you assert by becoming a victim."

She saw me shrink inwardly, my bruised hand reaching the side of my neck, where a thorn scratch had formed a tiny scab, a comma.

"Tell me I'm wrong," she said.

"Of course you are."

"Promise me," she said.

"Of course I promise you," I said, outmaneuvering my sister just slightly.

Cass found her way to a white iron chair, practically glowing in the dark. Dad wanted to replace the wrought iron with teak.

"You and Danny have had a fight," I suggested.

She slumped pointedly in the chair like someone protesting uncomfortable furniture. "Danny wouldn't dare fight with me," she said.

The other night Cass had threatened to tell Mother an ugly thing about Dad. Sometimes I wondered what it was like to be married, to care so much about someone, but not really know what they were doing when they were away from home.

"Do you miss the days," I asked, "when we had the apartment by the creek?"

"That dumpy place," she said.

"Dad turned the television into a computer monitor," I continued, "and wrote his menus with us looking up words in the Italian dictionary."

And then Dad spoke, calling to us. The real Dad, not the man in our memory, asking where was everybody. He was close to us, having drifted in his ambling, possessive way, surveying the plants.

But for a moment he didn't see us, and we waited, like it was a game, Dad unaware of our presence.

chapter

14

The phone rang the first thing the next morning, right after I ran six fast miles on Dad's running machine. I had slept badly, waking so many times I had at last given up and watched TV with the sound off.

I don't like working out on a speeding conveyor belt, red digits counting the distance in kilometers, reckoning in miles if I pushed a button. It routinely calculated how many calories I was burning off, if I were a one-hundred-and-sixty pound, forty-two-year-old male. Still, you get the exercise done, and I had not wanted to go outside that morning, the dark-before-the-dawn too dark.

My hand was eager to pick up the phone by reflex. I like answering the phone—I can't help it. Only as I lifted the instrument to my ear did I think, It's Detective Margate.

So I said hello with the phone not very close to my head, creeping up on the conversation.

It was a male voice, with none of that cop weight.

It was Quinn. He sounded different after all these

months, his voice deeper and even more cautious than I recalled, so my heart didn't stop all at once.

"Jesus, it *is* you!" I said after he had talked for about half a minute, a prepared speech—Quinn is one of those people so sincere he can't think of what to say all at once.

"My dad's coming to Richmond this afternoon, on business, and I thought I'd like to drop by and see you." I guessed that this, too, was a memorized statement, but then he said, spontaneously, "I'm worried about you, Jennifer."

"Nothing to worry about," I said. I gave *about* extra weight, maybe adopting Quinn's cadence. I wondered if he imagined me surrounded by fluffy lace pillows, a maid bringing me tea on a tray. His father had won and lost fortunes. Quinn and his dad thought about money all the time.

"You know what anger is," said Quinn, the sort of empathic, half ironic thing that can make him hard to understand.

"I have heard of it," I said.

"Well, so you know how I feel."

We had agreed months before that our relationship was becoming way too steamy, and that since his father was taking a job running a casino in the Biggest Little City in the World, we should not be in contact any more.

It had worked, sort of. Out of sight, Quinn had faded, kept artfully in a mental upper room where I never looked.

But it all came back, every feeling.

Conures have a whistle that sounds like a steel roof being torn in two. Even an African gray, a phlegmatic, observant bird, can shriek like a fighter jet when he hears water trickling or music thumping on the radio.

Mr. DaGama was arguing with a man at the counter. Mr. DaGama had taught me that the customer is always right, even when he isn't. This customer, a thin man in a blue T-shirt, was complaining that the new cowhide leash he had bought had bite marks in it. Mr. DaGama was uncharacteristically adamant in explaining the obvious—that the leash had teeth marks because a dog had bitten the leather, "leaving the marks of teeth."

"I expected a quality product," said the blue T-shirt.

The parrots must have picked up the tension, because all of them began yelling in the back room.

"Get another leash off the rack, no charge," said Mr. DaGama from behind the counter, with an attempt at graciousness.

"I wanted a full refund," said Blue T-shirt. But you could tell the man was growing uncertain. Mr. DaGama has dark eyes and broad shoulders; he has no trouble throwing seventy-five pound bags of wild bird seed down from the truck.

There is a sign above the counter, tacked to a shelf among the profile shots of lorikeets and hyacinth macaws. EXCHANGES WITHIN TEN DAYS—NO CASH REFUNDS. Mr. DaGama raised his eyes upward to indicate the sign, which was located above and behind him. He looked like a man in the act of praying.

"All right, all right," the man said. Despite what he was saying he wrapped the leash around his hand, like he was going to protect his fist in a fight. He said "All right," a third time, not like he was agreeing, but like he was wise to some crime.

I hurried between the two men, unhitched a double-ply

leash from the rotating rack, and pressed it into Blue T-shirt's unencumbered left hand. "This is a new kind of leash, a new model just released, way better," I said.

Mr. DaGama put his hands flat on the counter.

"Strong?" asked the T-shirt man, but I could tell he would have accepted anything to get out of there.

"So strong you won't believe it," I said.

"You run an animal shop, you can't take two-week holidays," said Mr. DaGama, squeezing an eyedropper of bird antibiotic into Byron's water dish. "I never wanted to take a vacation, before now."

Byron's crest shuddered happily upward in response to the attention, but his stools were green water. He had been sleeping with both feet wrapped around a perch. Birds sleep on one leg or the other, a two-legged sleeper is in trouble. The veterinarian from down the street had recommended a double dose of medicine and admired our heat lamp and the air humidifier. "You're doing everything you can," the vet had said.

"Everybody needs to take a break from their routine," I said, feeling smart in a housewifey way.

"I have never come so close to losing my temper," said Mr. DaGama.

Byron yawned.

"This is very good!" said Mr. DaGama. "A yawn is a sign of normal sleepiness!"

This seemed to me like a slim reason for celebration, but I went out into the shop to tell Marta that Byron was yawning. Marta was stuffing sprays of millet seed into a paper bag.

I wanted to avoid Mr. DaGama for a little while. He had been stern with people since hearing about the attack on me the day before, although pointedly kind to me. He told me to take all the breaks I needed, and moved a chair into the back room in case I felt like sitting down. But even dogs brought in for a shampoo and trim sensed his mood, nervously quiet as he gave them a pat on the head.

"That's progress," Marta was saying. "Byron is doing better."

Millet is a pretty seed. It grows on stalks like plumes of grain, amber yellow. The trouble is that seeds fall off the stalk every time you touch it, so preparing a package of millet stalks takes care.

I helped Marta, bundling the stalks, running tape around the protruding stems, $1.49 per package, a good buy. All the Amazon family of parrots love it, eating the seeds with avid expressions.

"Mom says any time you want to dive Monterey she'll pack the wet suits," said Marta. "Tomorrow, or next week, any time you feel the need."

I could use a dive now, the growing pressure of the deep water in my ears, sunlight falling upward as I sank.

Sometimes when you bag up parrot seed—open a seventy-five pound wholesale sack, and weigh it out into smaller quantities—you run across moths. The insects live and breed in the big bags of dried corn kernels and pumpkin seed. I hate to kill them, and so does Marta, so we let them drift upward, gray fluttery creatures.

I didn't tell her I had talked to Quinn.

chapter

15

I like the fragrance of the Hair Now! shampoo doctored to smell like papaya or coconut. Even the chemical-warfare scent of dye and hair-straighteners smells fresh and clean to me.

Some haircutters engage in talk, gesturing with their scissors, agreeing with their clients, nice to see the sun, we sure need this rain. Paula cuts and observes, saying little. I sat obediently in her padded chair, and she didn't say anything, surveying my image in the mirror. She waits before she goes to work, a sculptor studying the clay.

She lifted up various portions of my tresses and said, "How long since you were here?"

"Two months?" It had been three, at least. I never get it very short, just freshen up the ends and let it be.

She pinched bird fluff off the back of my head and held it up.

I told her I was in a little bit of a hurry, a luncheon date, actually saying the word "luncheon," like I would be wearing white gloves.

"Oh, one of *those*," said Paula, tilting back her head to study my follicles through her reading glasses.

I tilted back in the shampoo chair, and she said, "A little more," tilted farther, and she said, "More," and at last, "I thought you were in a hurry." I was all the way back, and stared up at the black blades of the ceiling fan. I can never fit my neck in the right way into the crescent in the sink.

The scissors sounded loud, right next to my ear, an unsettling *hush hush* of steel blades, and by the time Paula was done, snips of my hair were all over the shiny tile floor.

I sprinted, fast even for me, but an unfamiliar red car was already parked in the driveway. This strange auto looked rakish and dangerous, the kind of car a cop is always pulling over.

He was in the kitchen. I took my time in the hall, listening to him talk about tomatoes. They were growing some in their back yard, he was saying, fertilizer mixed in with desert sand.

"I want Mr. Thayer to let me grow tomatoes," said Bernice. "All these flowers—what good are they? Try to eat a hydrangea."

Quinn tried to avoid argument, but I could sense him disagreeing, not wanting to, considering his words. "Some people like flowers," he offered.

"Earth is for food," said Bernice, sounding more military than ever.

This sort of nervousness was what had made my mother quit music school, this painful anticipation. Maybe I had inherited both my father's headaches and my mother's nerves. I twisted my blouse front in my hands, stylish navy blue shorts, cotton top, American-girl styling, made in Milan. I let the door open, made my entrance, my hair feeling light around my head.

I could hardly bear to sit across from him at a table set with Bernice's idea of late lunch, fresh peaches, a bowl of pears, fresh crusty bread, and a wedge of a yellow cheese with tiny pinhead bubbles. Salmon flesh, boned and formed to a picture-book fish shape, sweated oil on a platter beside tufts of fennel and corkscrews of lemon.

We made a show of eating, Quinn taller and darker haired, which surprised me. You wouldn't think hair could change color in a half a year. His face broke into all the familiar angles when he laughed. He took pleasure the way a dog does, no deceit or disguise in his emotions.

I caught a view of my head in the side mirror behind the row of goblets, if I stood up a little. Perky, shorter, and more full-bodied, somehow this hairstyle made me look wide awake.

He agreed that my family finally had enough room, and that all we needed in the garden was an airport. "Is your mom going to quit work?" he asked.

"What for?"

"Your dad must be oozing money," said Quinn. "You touch him and dollars squirt."

You couldn't eat the just-baked whole wheat without two-handing it, breaking bread, literally, crumbs all over the table. I finally decided to put on a wrestling-league performance, grunting theatrically, giving a cheer of self-congratulations when a chunk of the loaf tore free. Bernice stepped into the lunch nook, peering and asking if we needed anything.

"It's delicious," said Quinn. Then he added, "We're just happy."

Bernice didn't say a thing for a long moment, and then she lifted the corners of her mouth in a smile like nothing I had seen from her before.

I said the car looked good, and Quinn said, "Dad leased it."

The car was red-carpet red, a shade that looked flashy and courtly all at once, a BMW that seemed to vibrate with power even before you stuck in the key. It was a show-off auto, the kind a junior exec buys with his first raise even if he could never dine out again. I could hear Dad's voice saying that Andy, Quinn's dad, had always been the hottest dog in the West.

"Your dad is surviving," I offered, really just making conversation.

"He keeps ahead of the avalanche," said Quinn, shifting gears, not eager to discuss his father.

Andy McGowan designed the smiling deck, the playing cards that I gather are standard now in Tahoe and Reno. It looks like a traditional deck of playing cards, but the face cards are smiling pleasantly, the king benign, the queen glad, the jack just as jolly as can be. I play solitaire and eights, leaving games to other people. But I knew it was a startling innovation when Andy ordered these cards for the North Bay casino where pai-gow and lo-ball poker were the only type of legal gambling. It ignited Andy's success, and now he ran a casino in Nevada and had his picture taken with singers and lieutenant governors.

"I guess he'll never change," I said. It was my attempt at changing the subject, sounding merely politely interested.

"He's going to drop dead one of these days," said Quinn, after considering for a moment.

"You mean—he has enemies."

"Enemies?"

"People who want to take him for a ride out into the desert."

Quinn shook his head, laughing quietly, coming to a careful stop at a crosswalk, a man with an aluminum walker fording the street. "You always want life to be more exciting than it really is," said Quinn.

He was wearing sharp-creased chinos and dark brown loafers, but I had known him when he was lucky to have frayed jeans and a polo shirt. His father had hungry ex-wives, including Quinn's mom, drifting in and out of travels with a string of broad-shouldered men in their twenties. Quinn's dad gave away envelopes of money for Christmas, ordinary Woolworth white envelopes with brand new hundred dollar bills.

The BMW leaped up the hill and down the dirt road, coming to a stop in the eucalyptus shade.

I told Tommy Dixon I wasn't ready to take Flower for a "spot of exercise," we just wanted to look.

"Jennifer, when you feel ready, we're ready," said Tommy. He meant we the wranglers, we the horses, as though he could speak for Flower, the animal excited, practically tap-dancing on the hoof-powdered earth. He could even speak for the bearded goat tethered beside the stables.

I used to come up here when I was twelve and thirteen, drape my arms on the corral rails, and watch hour after hour while Tommy or his wife put a new filly through its paces, the jump barrier a little higher each time, until the world had another horse that could fly over the candy-stripe-painted pole, hover in midair. Tommy looks like a cowhand, but about half the owners prefer English style riding, jodhpurs and riding crops, and Tommy boarded some of the race horses for Golden Gate Fields. Tommy could wear a business suit, a top hat, a caveman outfit, and he would be the same jaunty guy, horses cocking their ears toward his step.

Tommy made me feel a little embarrassed, squinting at me from under his good-guy Stetson, ivory-gray, shading his eyes. The squint was fake, or habit. He could see me fine, a young woman with a new hairdo, standing next to the only person in the world she had ever had sex with.

I felt that Tommy, with his kind, knowing eye for animals could see all of this. I was standing right next to Quinn, but we weren't touching, Quinn offering polite, offhand comments, "These sure are beautiful animals."

"What are you going to do with Desert Flower?" Quinn was asking, one leg up on the corral. It must be in the genes, when a man approaches a railed fence, one leg goes up. I tend to put both arms over one of the top slats, and lean or hang.

"Teach her to read a wine list. What do you mean *do*?"

"She's just—" He had to finish the thought silently, eyebrows, eyes, his entire face saying, She's too lively, too wonderful, too expensive.

"It's taking some getting used to," I said.

He laughed.

We strolled around the stables. The goat looked but didn't touch at first, wary of us with its keyhole eyes. Quinn gave it a pat, and the goat nuzzled upward, the crook of his arm, the fly of his pants.

"Horses like goats," I said.

"Goats are nice," said Quinn, absently.

"I bet you're the only person in world history who ever said that."

"I guess the horses feel calm around goats," said Quinn, a little defensively. He was great with household animals, Scotties and kittens. He sounded like a westerner, but he knew vastly more about fuel injection motors than saddles.

"But nice means—nice. Polite and nonthreatening."

"You felt threatened by that goat?"

I conceded with a laugh—we had just paid a call on a goat trained to the point of niceness.

He stuffed his hands into his pockets. I could tell Quinn was getting ready to say something. I could live without hearing it.

chapter

16

"A skunk print," said Quinn, indicating a henlike scratch on the path.

"Maybe one of those rabid animals you hear about," I said. I was going to forestall Quinn forever.

We had walked up-slope, and looked back down on Sandalwood Ranch, corrals and spirited horses, the goat a tiny figure.

He said, "My dad hates Reno."

"I thought he was Mr. Wonderful in Reno, all those poker games you said went night and day."

"Everyone is so grumpy in Nevada."

I laughed.

"It's true. They get wrinkled faces by the time they're twenty-five from walking around with bad expressions."

"People are supposed to be the same everywhere," I said, knowing it wasn't true.

"When I heard about the thing that happened to

you—" He reached up and swiped at an overhanging oak branch, hit it hard, acorns too green to fall off.

Guys will stand together silently, watching an empty street. Quinn is like that, too, but you know he's thinking something.

"I'm going to get Dad to move back here," he said.

That's the trouble with Quinn—he makes these simple statements, and you know he means them.

He continued, "I'll tell Dad it isn't working out. He already figures as much."

"He has a career."

"He hates the people he sees every day. Pit bosses and dealers, and this greeter the casino has who used to be a sparring partner to some famous heavyweight. The greeter walks out to cars and says how good it is to see people again, come on in."

"What's wrong with that?"

"This boxer touches women. I mean, he touches them on purpose, like it's an accident. I think he messes with underage girls, and the casino buys off the parents. Dad says he's never seen such phony stupid people in his life. He says the phony smart ones in California were bad enough." Quinn's father and mine had been pleasant to each other, but I suspect Mr. McGowan considered Dad a food snob.

"You could go live with your mother."

"She's in London. We're moving back here in six months, at the latest. I'll talk Dad into it. I realized something."

I was supposed to ask, so I did.

"About you," he said.

I stepped to one side to avoid a tossing branch. I asked, "What are you doing?"

"Climbing."

The oak tree swayed and complained, Quinn elbowing up through the branches, higher. He grinned down at me and made a show of peering out at the view, whaler fashion. "I see your horse," he said.

"What's she doing?"

"She's saying, 'Damn, Jennifer's afraid of me.'"

Desert Flower was saddled, bridled, shaking her head, her mane a blur. Tommy made a little bow: She's all yours.

Quinn leaned against the stable, arms folded, under the shade of an eave to avoid the full afternoon sun.

I put my foot in the stirrup and wrapped my hands around the pommel. My running shoe looked puny and technological, white-and-black nylon contrasting with the dark, honest leather of the stirrup. I took a breath, gave myself a mental run-through, all the things I had learned and forgotten about riding.

I swung my leg up, and I was in the saddle.

Desert Flower turned to observe me, her copper-yellow eye looking me up and down, at my bare legs, and the white tape I wrap around my shoelaces. Her skin jumped and twitched, and she shifted her hooves from position to position, heaving, blowing out a huge breath. I gripped the reins hard, my fingers white around the leather.

"Looking good," called Quinn.

It's hard to look devil-may-care when you're trembling.

Desert Flower lifted a hoof, snuffled around, doglike, blasting flecks of golden straw with her exhaled breath, and then she skimmed forward, trotting, but not like any horse I had ever handled before. She traveled sideways, angling to the right, she jigged a little, and trotted sideways to the left. She stopped. I wasn't doing anything to direct the horse, just sitting in the saddle, Quinn giving me one of his wise, reassuring half smiles.

Tommy Dixon was tucking his head, so I couldn't see his grin, if that's what it was. He looked like an aw-shucks movie cowboy, looping a rope into tighter circles. I gave a toss of my head, and Tommy, perceiving through some form of ESP, made his move to the gate, swung it open.

And we were out.

The horse did what she wanted, kicked, sneezed, sneezed again, and then I made the mistake of urging her, with the *click, click* between my teeth the way I used to on that faraway summer when I was an eighth grader, Marta pounding ahead on a horse she was working into a lather.

With most horses you go from a trot to a stiff-legged pace to a happy canter, and then, if you aren't heading uphill, the horse rocks into a gallop, grunting and panting, saddle girth creaking.

Desert Flower skimmed along the ground, my shadow rippling over blurred roots and stones, a dry creek, a scatter of leaves like coins, a field of white-yellow oat weeds. I hung on.

And I began to think, Time to slow.

Time to slow down. We were rushing onward toward a tangle of low-hanging oaks, and I pressed my face into the horse's mane and said, "Slow down."

Maybe the words sounded enough like *whoa.* The mare didn't slow, exactly, but she did cant her body sideways, like someone turning back while they keep running, trying to hear what a friend is calling.

I fell off.

Once. Desert Flower was loping down a rocky creekbed, and I slid forward and out of the saddle. I hopped one-footed along the creek gravel. The horse was curious—maybe the skittering of the stones caught her eye. Maybe she was being patient, but I think she didn't care either way, whether I was off or on.

Quinn ran through the brush, stopping to catch his breath. He couldn't talk when he saw me, only lift his arm and bend over, breathing too hard.

I was back in the saddle by then, ducking under a branch. Flower found something about Quinn's arrival interesting, stretching her head out in his direction although he was still a stone's throw away.

Quinn reached, reached again. The horse shied from his touch, then allowed him to caress her at last.

chapter

17

"I like it," said Mom, meaning my hair.

"Functional," I said.

"Cute," she said.

I expected her to continue, selecting the right compliments, that it had bounce. Mom gets into these moods, when she needs small talk like a drug. There was dust between my teeth, in my ears.

Quinn had asked if there was some place we could go, but I said I had to hurry back. I was surprised at how I felt, unable to tell him that I had deceived everyone. I knew Quinn would not be here except for my lie.

Mom folded her arms and said, "Detective Margate called."

"What about?" I asked, my legs a little stiff from the saddle. I wanted a shower, my Quinn-glow fading.

"We aren't supposed to tell anyone: Oakland Police are about to make an arrest."

My throat closes when I feel too much all at once. Dad has the same problem. I gave the little cough I copied from him, half nervous habit, half necessity. "They're about to catch someone?"

"According to Margate."

"Who is he?"

She shook her head: I don't know. "People have been calling," she said. "Friends crawling out of the woodwork. They know what happened. People talk."

I found it a little troublesome to breathe but kept at it, the way you do twenty meters down, trusting your equipment.

She shifted a finger, got a better grip on her elbow. "I called Dr. Yellin."

Dr. Yellin, my mom's psychiatric hero. She had taken a course from him, and he had written on her paper a giant pink "Brava!" She thought he was the wisest man on the planet.

"I want to help the police, if I can," I said, not putting enough power into the words.

"I think you've been through enough," she said. "I have my doubts about you going down to the police department for the lineup, all those detectives getting their hooks into you."

My voice said, "I only heard a few words."

Wait a minute.

"It wouldn't be a visual lineup, in your case. They might even have the spoken words on tape, Margate tells me. But she pleads for our cooperation."

"Tonight?"

"She wants to see you now. She wants to review the

case. We have to be reasonable." Mom was doing her usual form of pacing, standing in one corner, delivering a few words, appearing in another part of the room, uttering a few more. It must be some old opera training, keeping the audience entranced while she tried to hit those high Cs.

Mom was trying to convince herself, so I kept my mouth shut.

"We want to help," she was saying. "Up to a point. The TV and newspapers don't know the case is going to break. Margate says Berkeley PD can sit on the news a day or less, but then the Oakland police blotter and the DA's office will leak once they grab the guy, no matter what. She wants to review your options."

"What does that mean?"

Mom acts in control but puts too much effort into it, arranging magazines on the coffee table, straightening pillows on the sofa. I knew that if Cass told my mother about Dad it would hurt.

"There must be something distinctive about the suspect's voice," Mom went on. "Something only you would know. An accent, a lisp, some special quality. You can help the cops nail this guy, the way no one else can." She hesitated, waiting for me to chime in with a description of the voice.

Wait a minute. I imagined the words spoken in different voices: a rasp, a musical tenor, a Daffy-Duck sputter.

"She says then it will be hard to keep your identity a secret. No one will print your name, but everyone will know without saying. If they can keep the man in custody without your testimony, they'll do it."

"So I won't have to testify," I said.

"You probably will, at the preliminary hearing, but they can do it through deposition. They'll seek to protect your identity because you're a minor."

"I'll be one of those talking silhouettes. Like those ex-CIA agents who tell all to the news."

"I called Marcell Springer. He said freeze-dry you, talk to a head doctor, and keep you out of the picture."

I recognized the name of Mom's old lawyer friend, the one who helped her beat the speeding ticket. I also recognized his choice of words. But I would do anything before I spoke with Dr. Yellin, Mom's own personal psychological Buddha. "So—what's the difference, if everybody knows," I said.

"Jennifer," she said: Don't be an idiot.

"I'll be respected," I said, finally getting some electricity into my voice. "I'll be an example to women, not to be afraid."

"That's not the way to handle this," she said.

"What if the suspect won't cooperate?" I said.

"I told her no way would I subject you to an ordeal," said my mother. "I said we would seek our own medical counsel before we made a move."

"This guy they are about to arrest is going to say 'Wait a minute'? Like he's auditioning for a play. Step forward and sound like a rapist, Mr. Doe. That doesn't make any sense. Why would a criminal say something in a lineup, like he's happy to be able to help. What kind of lawyers does this poor guy have?"

"He might be innocent," said my mother.

For a moment I thought, My mother doesn't believe me.

But then she continued, "All I want to do is protect you, Jennifer. I would love to go back in time and erase this, like it never happened."

Maybe they won't catch the suspect, I thought. Maybe he's thrusting his dirty socks and K-mart denims into a bag, leaving for the other side of the world.

"Where's Dad?"

"He's on his way."

The Southwest Air 11:05 from L.A. was one of my dad's favorite flights, always half empty, and he could pick whatever seat he wanted.

"I saw a robbery once," Mom was saying, "on the sidewalk, when I was younger than you." I knew the story well, but now this legend from my mother's past really mattered. "It was in downtown Oakland, on Telegraph Avenue, a big man with a sawed-off baseball bat knocking down a man carrying a briefcase."

She could see it now, after all this time, and she wished she couldn't.

It was one of those stories people tell over and over. Sometimes you don't want to hear them, sometimes you do. "Police had me sitting in the police station looking at mug shots, and for years I'd dream about those black-and-white photos, those grim, tired, hard-looking men."

It was like she was telling me this for the first time. "I'd dream I was looking at a row of faces," she said, "and they came to life. They moved their lips. They frowned. One by one they moved their eyes. And looked right at me."

When the doorbell made its ding-dong, a computer chip programmed to sound like iron bells, Mom gave me a reassuring smile.

I crept upstairs. I shut my bedroom door quietly but firmly and stood beside the jamb. The house was big, and the walls were thick. The faintest murmur seeped through to me, Detective Margate's consonants, her s's sharp, like a badly tuned radio.

I pressed my skull against the doorjamb, but the vague, simmering murmurs would not distill into words. Months from now people would pass me in corridors and whisper, She helped the police break the case. She fought off the attacker.

When people knew the truth about me, all this would vanish.

chapter

18

My mother writes exams for software companies, tests designed to cull crooks and risk-lovers. To the statement "You like a lot of excitement in your life," the correct answer is *No*. If you check *Yes* beside "You like to drive fast sometimes, just for fun," you'll end up working somewhere else.

Some of these tests are administered face to face, jobseeker and psychologist. I took some of these exams, trying them out, cueing Mom when a question was too obvious. No one wanting a job would answer *yes* to, "I have been in shouting matches with my boss."

When you lie, sometimes your eyes look upward, at the questioner's eyebrows. Sometimes your foot gives a little kick, unconsciously booting the question away. Listen for the pauses in the examiner's voice, Mom always said.

The tests are so easy I'm surprised anyone ever fails.

The detective stayed a longer time than I expected, like someone returning a borrowed book, saying they loved the ending, no time for any decaf, but then lingering anyway, to talk about their favorite chapter, the one where the murderer blurts the truth.

Afterward, my mother tapped on my door with her fingernails and said, "She's overworked." She wrinkled her nose as she said this, meaning, Just between you and me. "Her husband is a contractor—he remodels kitchens. They both want to have children."

My mother asks, and people talk.

"She hates this attacker, whoever he is. Personally. She wants to see him rot on a meat hook. She says the Oakland police are staking out an apartment building on Fruitvale Avenue."

"What did she say about him?"

"She said the suspect has been in and out of institutions for thirty years."

"Institutions?" Not jails, not prisons. "A violent man," I ventured.

"She says he's sugar to everyone, nice-nice, until he gets a woman alone."

A sick feeling throbbed inside me.

"I said you weren't here," Mom added.

"Did she believe you?"

Mom makes a quiet, pretty laugh through her nose, as though too courteous to laugh out loud.

"Are you sure she isn't watching the house?"

"You're as bad as Cass." My sister had done a report on

the CIA as a high school senior, and for months afterward was pointing out innocent-looking pedestrians who could be operatives.

"I'll have a talk with Dad," she said. She usually referred to my father as Terry or Terrance.

I took a ten-second shower, toweled off, and skimmed into my nightie. I turned out my light. I was sure I could see the dim strobe of an emergency blinker, the cops sitting at the curb conferring. I stole across the floor and parted the drapes. The street was empty.

Plumbing whispered quietly in a far corner of the house, my mother taking a bath or a shower, trying to quiet her mind so she would be able to sleep. The phone trilled beside me and I groped, knocked it off the bed, found it in the dark.

Cass gets affectionate and talky when she's sleepy. She asked how I was feeling, was I getting enough rest, and then, niceties observed, careened right into her usual topic A. She said Danny found everything too easy, he rarely even had to study.

I said that this was hard for people like Cass and me to understand, because our own parents had worked so hard. Cass had always complained about Danny, said he was too good looking and that he was always going off to embassy cocktail parties with his parents, meeting God knew what sort of French-speaking temptress. It was her way of bragging.

"Well, Dad didn't exactly suffer," Cass began.

"Remember how he didn't want us to see how upset he was when the restaurant burned?"

Cass had picked up a knowledge of sleeping pills from one of her first boyfriends, a pre-med student with an MG. I wondered if she had been mixing a few sleepy-time tablets with a glass of wine. For an instant I worried, thinking: Barbiturates, alcohol, coma.

Cass was making her feline sound of a person mulling heavy ideas, not to be interrupted. A yawn, or half yawn, flared the silence. "It's true—there were tears in his eyes," she said.

I found myself thinking how much easier it would be on Dad if the wedding was called off.

I looked dumpy in my maid-of-honor dress, a robin's-egg blue Dupioni silk V-neck with a sweeping, A-line skirt. I didn't look cavewoman, but I didn't look half as good as Cassandra did in her princess-line skirt, off-the-shoulder bodice, white all the way. The wedding consultant had told Dad this was the glamorous but understated look an afternoon wedding demanded.

I had expected the consultant to be a friendly Dracula, eager to watch the fittings, all of us in our undies. Instead he had the carelessly well-dressed manner of a basketball coach and talked about *flow:* traffic, caterers. "Attention wants to flow to the bride."

"I'd have a heart attack," she continued, "rather than call off the wedding. If we agreed to get divorced right after the ceremony, we're going through with it, no matter what." A brace of her Stanford friends, willowy and talkative, were going to be stunning as bridesmaids, a court of powder-blue dresses.

"Dr. Theobald is going to recite a poem," I said.

As she sometimes does when approached by news she

dislikes, she checked her hearing, made sure her data was sound before she reacted. "Dr. Theobald is doing *what?*"

I told her again, same words, same tone of voice.

"I didn't agree to that."

"Dad left me a note, like it's especially wonderful news."

She didn't sound sleepy now. "I told Dad that Dr. Theobald is unreliable." She said his name with mockingly overcorrect pronunciation *Tib-buld*. "I don't even like the way his voice sounds when he reads."

"It doesn't say what poem. But Dad used three exclamation points."

"My God, what if Dr. Theobald *wrote* this poem and he's going to recite it out loud." She was wide-awake—I could almost hear the sheets slithering off her.

It would be easy to think that Cass had picked Danny out of a catalog, a glossy sampler of handsome guys sure to make bucks. She met him at a Monday Night Football party in Palo Alto, the pony keg nearly empty. They had volunteered to go out for more Miller Lite, and they missed the second half, never came back with so much as a bag of pretzels. Danny believed in God, could read German, and had once owned a budgie named Fatty. He told me he'd teach me how to play five-card draw, and every time he saw me he asked how Marta was doing, was I still running.

I was imagining demanding sexual practices, urgent appetites. "Danny's used to having everything his way," Cass said, not about to be bought off with a change of subjects.

I sensed that I was trespassing, but tiptoed ahead. "Danny's insistent," I hazarded.

Thinking about Danny calmed her, like he was a familiar bedtime story. "If I say I don't want halibut, it has those bones that scratch your throat, he just laughs and has the fish man weigh out the biggest halibut on ice."

"Danny cooks?"

"No, he expects me to bone this creature the size of a hog, because he thinks food runs in the family." The word *family* seemed to trigger associations. "Why is it," she asked, "neither you nor I can sing?"

It isn't very dark in my bedroom at night. Headlights stroke the blank ceiling, and when you sense someone downstairs you can lie awake thinking it's almost dawn, when it's just one A.M. I wondered how much more of this I could stand, waiting for everyone to discover the truth.

For a quiet house, this place makes a good deal of noise, gentle, rustling, whispering sounds, Dad home, Dad hungry. I was aching for sleep, thirsty for it. I lay there wide awake, thinking, Where would I go once they knew.

I got up way before dawn and sweated six miles on the machine in the cellar. The last half mile I upped the speed so fast that I was nearly thrown off the machine backward, the belt whining. Dad had tacked an alpine scene on the wall. You ran toward a snowy slope, a meadow bursting with green, flowers like yellow stars.

I bumped into Dad as he stood waiting his turn. He looked baggy eyed and worn. There was definite pudge around his middle inside his gray T-shirt. He says he puts on weight just holding his breath.

He started the machine but didn't get on it, the black belt humming along unoccupied. The machine burst into action at the speed I had previously set, and he looked at me with mock horror, leaning into the button until the machine was ticking along sedately, three miles an hour, nothing.

"Your mother and I had a chance to talk last night," he said, not getting on the machine yet. "She has a good idea."

"Mom is full of ideas."

"But this is one you'll like," he said, starting to run.

chapter
19

"I think it's just awful the police won't leave you alone," called Mrs. Emmit over the hum of the van. "They should leave you in peace."

Marta's dad swore at a truck that changed lanes too quickly. He cocked his head to yell into the back of the van, where Marta and I were swaying with the motion of the stop-and-go traffic. "You have to be a certain type of person to be a cop."

I felt a little defensive about my own two detectives, and offered, "They just try to do their job."

"No, they don't," said Mr. Emmit, ready to launch into a story about an officer he had seen bullying a homeless person, or maybe a meter maid with a snippy attitude. Mrs. Emmit said something, a sharp whisper, and Mr. Emmit put his shoulders up, like a turtle. "You're right, Jenny," he sang out. "They do their best."

This had been Mom's plan: a couple days out of town, and maybe the cops wouldn't need me after all.

The back of the van was a jumble of blue diving fins and Aqua Lung cylinders, heavy tanks of air. The diving masks were night-glow yellow, the Scubapro buoyancy compensator vests and wet suits perfect black. It looked like a squad of sea monsters had run afoul of the Emmits and paid a terrible price.

All the way down Highway 101 the Emmits were especially sensitive, asking me if I needed the window up, or maybe down a little more, and did I mind the radio on, KCBS jabbering the news. They finally turned the radio to some easy listening station at Mrs. Emmit's whispered prompting, the music you hear in the dentist's office, jazz musicians without any blood in their bodies.

During this drive it was never, "Is anyone hungry?" or "Anyone have to use the ladies'?" meaning did we need to pee. It was always, "How do you feel, Jennifer?" "Jennifer, need a soda?" They usually traveled along in a happy uproar, caught up in one of Mr. Emmit's anecdotes, actresses with laryngitis, actors with elevator shoes. Mrs. Emmit usually tossed the lunch into the farthest corner of the van and then had the passengers pass food forward all the way to Monterey, two or three hours, depending on traffic.

Today they were like hospital workers taking a celebrity madwoman out to see the scenery. I had never seen them so considerate, asking me if I was hungry, offering me a pillow for my head, as though I could not hold myself upright.

The drive to Monterey goes in three distinct stages as you head south from San Francisco Bay. First, there is urban damage, freeway construction and stucco houses, Fremont, San Jose.

Then, hills. They were dry now, in the middle of July, cows looking up-slope or downhill over yellow pastureland. The Emmit family always grew calm as they left this landscape behind, because they were finally reaching the point of it all, the gentle descent into a new countryside, rolling past the sand dunes toward the curve of Monterey Bay.

Their weekend house is in Pacific Grove, right at the Monterey city limit. It overlooks the heavy seaweed and sluggish surf of the Pacific, down a short, sandstone bluff blanketed with ice plants.

Because they visit only every few weeks, the front gravel always needs to be raked, and the back yard needs to be mowed. The Emmits immediately tore into every challenge the place offered, a cute wood-frame house, green with white trim. They aired out the garage, unlocked the basement, laid gardening tools in the driveway, a hoe and shears on a long handle.

Mrs. Emmit was a round, pretty woman, with red hair cut short. Mr. Emmit used to be an active stick-figure, all hurry, cursing with every step. Now he was mostly peaceful, on the latest nerve medication. He wanted to see me happy, turning the living room light off and on and off again as I unwound the vacuum sweeper cord. "Or leave it on," he asked me, hand on the switch.

"I'm all right," I said.

I never could get impatient with the Emmits. Besides, today I came to think that they saw something in me, a pallor in my skin, a weakness in my gaze, that I was only half aware of.

Marta asked, "Do you want to dive this afternoon, or wait?" She phrased it a couple of different ways, "We could suit up and head down there now. We could do it in the morning."

"Let's wait," I said.

"Sure," said Marta, as though I had guessed the winning answer.

Her family unpacked, saying I could have the back bedroom all to myself, the one with the brand-new mattress and a digital clock I could unplug if it made me nervous. "I hate waking at night and seeing the little dot blinking off and on," said Mr. Emmit, as though I would take comfort in hearing that other people had troubles, too.

Coverlets had to be shaken out, windows opened all the way, the bungalow reawakened for the weekend. While Marta and I swept dust mice out the back porch, I told her about Desert Flower.

I had wondered how I would bring up the subject, and now that I had started I told her about Quinn, too. Not in detail, reserving everything but the bare facts, folding up a multicolored quilt as I spoke, Marta giving me her full attention, holding her head sideways, like a dog eager for every sound.

Marta enjoys other people's good news. What kind of horse was it? she wanted to know. Who had trained her?

Had I seen her medical papers, and did I know anything about Flower's diet? What kind of tack did I have—saddle and bridle—and who was going to take care of the mare when I wasn't around?

It was easy to brush off Marta's questions, but I felt embarrassed for not knowing the answers, not having learned more. The horse was even now standing in the shadow of a stable, needing someone's company.

Marta was thrilled, so much to ask. When was Quinn's dad moving back to Oakland? Would they buy or rent an apartment? What had gone wrong in Reno? Was Quinn still going to go to a California college, or did he try for one of the Nevada schools? Did he still play basketball?

All I knew was because of my lie Quinn was a part of my life again.

Marta stopped asking, suddenly. She probably felt bad for talking so much, pestering a victim.

Lynn Emmit, Marta's mom, was a student set designer in the days when my mom was studying opera, and Mrs. Emmit still created sets for various theater groups up and down the West Coast. She drew pictures in idle moments, beautiful doodles, ballerinas and deer.

"Now I know this is ordinary macaroni," said Mrs. Emmit, scooping out noodles baked with cheese. Nothing like what you're used to, she implied.

"We eat pasta all the time," I said.

"What I do is freeze stuff before we head down, meat-loaf, chili, pack it into the Coleman cooler, and stick it in the microwave."

I knew her culinary methods, we all did. But the litany of how the Emmit family cooked their suppers in advance, and the admiration of the food as we ate, was a part of the comforting ritual of a visit to the bungalow. No, it didn't need any more salt. Yes, we would each have a second helping.

The surf was in the distance, huffing and puffing.

chapter

20

I had slept the night through, no dreams, and I wondered how long I could stay where I was.

My body made the decision to sit up, feet on the floor, standing, walking on autopilot. I parted the curtain, and cloudy morning brightness made me blink. House finches fluttered from branch to branch.

A hummingbird feeder hung from the tree. The feeder was always empty when the Emmits arrived, ignored by the aggressive, iridescent hummers. But they came back, loyal to their memory, even after weeks of nothing. The hourglass jar was full of ruby sugar water, two quick male hummingbirds sword-fighting in mid air.

I heard the Emmits in the kitchen, whispering.

Marta and I agreed that a lean breakfast was best before a dive. We each ate half a piece of dry toast. "Feeding the fish" was scuba lingo for throwing up underwater. It was an experience we both wanted to avoid.

I washed the few cups and dishes, while Mrs. Emmit used a worn dishtowel patterned with Shakespeare's face and the words THE PLAY'S THE THING. The dish soap smelled like lemon candy. The view out the kitchen window was a pine tree, syrupy sap beading the crook of a branch, a fishing boat chugging out to sea. The window was dirty with salt spray, and the view was hazy.

As we watched, Mr. Emmit's face appeared. He was squirting Windex and clearing the panes with a fistful of paper towels.

It was a little unusual, this two-person kitchen routine. My family either loads the washer or lets the dishes dry bare.

"I hear Cass finally picked a photographer," said Mrs. Emmit.

"She chose one months ago," I said. "But the man she wanted is on long-term assignment for *National Geographic*." It figured that Cass had wanted a wildlife photographer to snap her wedding.

"Oh my," said Mrs. Emmit, ready to console. Marta marched by with the shears on a pole, the tool for reshaping the branches of tall trees.

"The consultant recommended one," I said. Cass had said she wouldn't let ninety-nine percent of the photographers she reviewed take pictures of her autopsy. "Cass says he understands her vision."

"You have to learn," said Mrs. Emmit. Mrs. Emmit remembered our birthdays and gave us each a present for Christmas, but sometimes I didn't understand her.

"To listen," she added. "So you can give people what they want. Sometimes I'm sitting there with my colored pencils and my sketch pad, all ready to create a set design for a play, and the director doesn't have a clue!"

"Cass has a good idea she wants a garden wedding, with a string quartet and the sun shining." Somewhere outside the shears snipped.

"At least you don't have to read Cass's mind," said Mrs. Emmit.

I fished for the old-fashioned plug, a rubber stopper with a ring. I pulled the plug ring, and the sink gave a pleasant gurgle. I like to take a moment and rinse out the skein of suds clinging to the sink, splashing everything away.

"A friend of mine wants to write an article about you," said Mrs. Emmit, hesitation in her voice. "Ruthie Deerborn writes for one of those weekly newspapers everybody reads. Full of stories about interesting people." Her voice rose upward, like a question, but not.

My expression must have encouraged her.

"She's excited about the way you defended yourself," she said. "When you hear about something like that, we all want to stand up and cheer."

It would have been easy for someone to look at me and think, She's embarrassed, but pleased.

"That would be all right, wouldn't it?" said Mrs. Emmit. "Sharing what happened with the public?" She put her damp hand on mine. "We wouldn't have to use your name, Jennifer. Only your friends would know."

• • •

I stretched my wet suit on the front yard gravel and examined the connectors, early morning low cloud burning off. Most divers don't like to expose their suits and masks to any more full sun than they have to—it dries out vinyl.

Marta joined me, two mad scientists with humanoid body parts. "Soon they walk the earth," said Marta, sounding just like the German biology teacher at our school.

I worked the purge button, to make sure the action was clear, and did what Mr. Emmit always recommended—blew through all connectors, just to make sure a spider or a moth hadn't tucked himself in. It had been too long since I had been down, and I kept tightening and loosening my mask strap, making sure it fit.

chapter

21

I always feel ridiculous just before I enter the water in that Halloween diving getup. Everything made a science-fiction noise, my feet squelching sand with each step.

Marta made it look natural in her black-and-yellow gear, her eyes alert behind the lens of her mask. She waded into the sea, slipped her fins on, then ducked her head under the surface, taking that first, wonderful look below. Then she treaded water, took the mouthpiece from between her teeth, and said, "Take your time."

I wet the inside of my mask with a little water, cooling the inside of the lens so it wouldn't mist up. I rubbed some spit inside the lens, too. I made a point of going slow, feeling nervous. This was unusual. I had always loved diving. But they talk about the premonition you have hours before a moray eel takes a chunk out of your shin.

Marta lolled in the waves and then swept her arm around, rolling in one beautiful motion into the water. She resurfaced and churned along through the clots of seaweed, picture perfect, waiting for her diving buddy. The kelp is thick, and she made sure I carried a knife on my belt to slash my way free if I got tangled. It was a stainless steel weapon, with four round finger holes in the grip.

I tested the knife for feel, thrusting, cutting the air. The Aqua Lung hung awkwardly on my back, like an artillery shell I just happened to have slung over my shoulder.

Mr. Emmit had backed the van all the way to the overhang. He was strapping on his gear, ready to join us in a few minutes.

The pier to my left carried a scattering of tourists out into the bay, while the boutiques and restaurants of Cannery Row glittered in the morning sun, parked cars and window washers, land folk going about their business. Seals jammed together at the end of the pier, a pile of brown sleeping bags.

This is the most awkward time, when you are not one of the land people anymore, and not a water creature, either. I put my hand on my regulator valve, test twisted it for a second, and then put my hands to my head and pulled hard, stretched the mask strap, forcing the diving mask over my forehead, my eyes.

The strap had a twist in it, and I worked it free with my finger, a lock of hair adhering to the rubber, sticking to it, tugging—it hurt. I freed my hair, and felt the dull curiosity of the tourists, and thought I could make out the quack-quack of commentary, my body shapeless under the black suit.

Or not quite shapeless—you could tell I was female, and I felt vulnerable, trapped in my equipment. I envied

Marta, who was already far out, slapping the water loudly every now and then, an unspoken *Come on!*

I felt the subtle suction of the mask, smelled the latex and faint, salty zest of the interior of the mask as my heels kissed the water. We had taken our lessons in a University of California swimming pool in Strawberry Canyon, weeks of treading water, learning about ascent rates, how to avoid the bends.

I tasted the sharp, almost bitter flavor of the mouthpiece, rolled over onto my tummy, and there was the glittering, grainy surface of the ocean floor, an arm's length away, sand ripples and flecks of mica, and a quarter-moon of shell. I adjusted the regulator, and tasted the neutral everyday flavor of tanked air.

I kicked my fins, and the bottom fell away—sharply away—and the tall, streaming ribbons of kelp reached upward.

I was only a meter or two below the surface when a slow leak tongued my cheek, and a disc of glassy fluid jiggled and swayed in the interior of my mask.

It's the first thing you learn—how to clear a leak. I pressed my hand against the top of the mask and blew hard out of my nostrils. The leak was gone. Marta was a luminous sketch, the yellow of her wet suit glowing in the dark.

A layer of cold water swept up to me, and the ice-chill flashed through my wet suit, all the way to my flesh. And the leak began again, insistent, a spreading puddle quaking just below my eyes.

chapter 22

Starfish glowed, astonishing orange hands, hanging on to the boulders. Eye-catching colors, the glow of traffic cones and graffiti. I descended, forcing the leak from my mask with an effort, blowing hard through my nose.

Marta was on her feet, doing a graceful shimmy to stay where she was, indicating with her hands a bushel of sea urchins. This shock of urchins resembled five hundred tiny porcupines, gray-green. She was telling me to be careful—the urchin needles could break at a touch and fester in our skin.

I felt the impulse kneading my skull, massaging into me: Why ever leave this place?

The surface high up there was molten glass, broken by the silhouette of a human crab kicking forward without effort, Mr. Emmit enjoying the view. Marta glided along the crustacean-encrusted floor, her hands bottle-green in the transformed sunlight.

She was entering a kelp holdfast, and I followed.

Marta parted the way ahead, the trunks of the seaweed lofting upward, a coliseum of garden hoses straining toward the sky.

Mr. Emmit hovered middle depth, pointing the beam of a flashlight among the trellises of seaweed, content with trolling the water, easy and in no hurry. The sound in my ears was the rasp and suck of my breath, the muted thunder as bubbles ballooned upward, and the water-deformed sounds that never make sense—murmuring surf, the brilliant *chink* as Marta brushed a stone.

Something pushed me.

A body shrugged into me, knocked me aside, a shopper in a hurry, no time to apologize. A svelte, muscular presence silked around me, arcing, circling, massive and lithe at the same time. I could not make out what it was. A fin tossed upward, blocking my view.

Something in me wasn't afraid. Some strange, foreign part of me was relieved.

I crouched, pulling out from under the coursing body.

I kicked hard, pumping water with my fins, and the surface approached, the roiling, glassy lava, day and sky. I told myself to keep breathing—there was danger of a gray-out. I broke the ceiling, ripped the breathing piece from my mouth, and sucked real air.

The ocean burst beside me, and the sea-dragon shape of Marta joined me, wrenching at her mask.

Her eyes blinked at the sudden noon light, the mask leaving an indentation on her cheeks, a curved line.

"Something scared me," I gasped.

"I saw it," she said.

She didn't want to embarrass me.

"A seal, right?"

"A big one, though," she panted. "A really huge bull seal, with a definite bad attitude, I could tell."

A harbor seal—the mildest-tempered animal in existence. I stuffed the apparatus back into my mouth, cleared my mask with a snort, and surged downward again, looking for the killer beast.

The animal had startled me. But that wasn't what bothered me as I leg-beat my way down.

A shadowy portion of me had felt relief at the sudden weight as it brushed me. A voice in me had whispered, unafraid, like a voice giving a weather report, *So this is how it ends.*

I climbed downward as I tried to warn myself to go back, now.

chapter 23

The seal was gone, trailing along the surface far away.

Marta pulsed ahead, over a boulder bearded with fish, a school, tails up, swimming to stay in place, feeding on the green rock. A column of sunlight ascended from the sea floor.

My hand was on the plastic sheath of the mini knife fastened to my belt. I could slip the stainless steel knife, brand-new, and cut the air tube, watch the gas gush and bubble, boiling upward. All it would take would be that one nick.

I could stay here, taking deep breaths of cold water.

Some hitch in my stroke made the quivering surface recede above me, lifting higher as I swam toward it. Oxygen poisoning, my brain overloading, not enough nitrogen in the air.

. . .

You expect the surface to have a texture, roiling and smoothing. It looks like a silvery membrane. I broke it easily.

I can tread water by the hour, no effort. But now my breath was ragged, the sunlight cheap-bright. I was closer to the pier than I expected, the cylindrical timbers hairy with sea muck, the barnacles glittering, sharp edged.

The tide was dragging me slowly toward the columns of wood, the salt water seething, and I felt my arms and legs flail. I was strengthless, and I could not breathe.

Air gushed behind me, Marta sputtering, her mouth piece gurgling air and water. She put a hand out to me, while with the other she wrenched at her mask.

"A cramp?" she asked.

I gave a quick nod, coughing water. Salt water is pungent, iodine and alum, hot pepper and bitter salt. The tide was pushing us into the pier timbers. The water was black, sank fast, seething. It chuffed upward again in a flash, boiling white.

Marta took my arm, as though we were pretending: I'll rescue you. But it was only half pretend. For all her strength, I could tell that Marta was afraid, too—of the dark simmering under the pier. And afraid of what she saw in my eyes, a panic you read about but never believe can really happen.

Mr. Emmit grinned with the effort, pulling his webbed feet, slop, slop, out of the foam.

"Are you all right?" he asked.

"We're good," I said, sounding as casual as possible, doing it well.

"Jennifer got a cramp," said Marta.

Divers get cramps fairly often, from extending the long muscles of their legs in cold water. "It passed," I said.

Mr. Emmit dried his head with a faded green towel and tossed one over to Marta, the two of them scrubbing their heads until their hair stuck out all over. One of the problems with diving is the salt in your hair, thick glop that sticks every hair together.

The knife was gone, my hand touching the empty sheath.

chapter

24

Marta and I sat on the back steps, drinking hot chocolate, summer sunset finished.

Along the coast in the summer evenings clouds glide across the sky, stay all night, and burn off by noon. You can feel the dark rise right up out of the ground.

The hot chocolate tasted good, the heat of the hand-thrown, warty cups just what I needed. I had showered, using baby shampoo on my hair, and spent the afternoon watching the Emmits' videotapes, *Underwater Wonders of the Red Sea, Deep Water Diving off the Big Island.*

Marta slurped her chocolate pointedly, about to say something.

"You panicked," she said.

I did not want to ask myself why I had pulled the knife.

I spoke after a short silence. "I'll pay for a new one."

"You panicked. Twice." This was typical Marta, saying something and continuing to say it, hammering the point.

I kept quiet.

"I feel strange down there, too, sometimes," she confided. "That's why we go down. Because we don't belong there."

"You do fine," I said.

She dismissed the compliment with a flick of her hand. "Some divers like that out-of-sync feeling. I met a guy who goes free diving, without tanked air. So he can feel ecstatic apnea." She uttered the phrase with exaggeration, like she didn't approve of it, and added, "When you almost die you supposedly feel great."

That's all it had been, I thought. The diver's equivalent to vertigo. It can happen to anyone.

"What happened to you today makes me feel better," she said. "You can fight off the Jogging Rapist, but you're human." The touch of envy in her voice surprised me.

My mother told me that in listening to people you watch the way they hold their bodies, pay attention to their silences.

"Mom wants me to take a course in martial arts," Marta said at last. "There's a class starting at the Y."

Marta folded her arms, imagining a struggle, I guessed, picturing it vividly in her mind. She said, "An attacker would fling me like a rag doll."

"I doubt it," I said. I wondered what it would be like to tell Marta everything.

"I could never hit a guy, one punch, and have him back off."

The envy in Marta's voice was unmistakable now. She swung her fist, slow motion, like a boxer. I put my hand out, wrapped my fingers around her fist.

When she spoke again, she said, "You should let Ruthie interview you, that friend of Mom's. She's wonderful."

My breath caught. There was something out there. Some animal at the edge of the dark back garden.

"She raised three kids herself," Marta continued, "working as an electrician. She redid all the circuit breakers at the theater. She took journalism classes at night, and now she publishes articles in magazines. She says she'd love to meet you."

I put a finger to my lips and pointed.

The possum made his choice, running with a peculiar gait in our direction. He did not lope, like most four-legged animals, but ran side to side—right legs, left legs—locomoting into the dazzle of the porch light.

He peered up at us, his eyes pink glass, his hairfree snout the color of white crayon, a little dirty.

He vanished under the house.

Waking up a second morning isn't as magical. Your body already knows it will be somewhere else by night. The sun is bright outside curtains that you can't look through without thinking, Who knows when you'll stand here again?

"I scrambled some eggs," said Mrs. Emmit, puckering her nose, not sure I was an egg person.

My parents taught us to say good morning first thing and show enthusiasm for whatever the hostess plans for breakfast.

The entire Emmit family leaned on things, elbows on tables, hips on doorjambs, in no hurry. They pulled curtains shut, made sure the packets of hot chocolate were sealed in Tupperware. Everything in the bungalow was second best, the couch saggy, the easy chair slumped with use.

It's nice but embarrassing to see a family going through its friendly paces, Marta pretending to talk through the floor to the possum. She used a little Minnie Mouse voice I had rarely heard before, telling him that all possums should be gone by next time.

I could feel it in my sinews, the way my feet dragged, how badly I did not want to go home.

chapter

25

We took a different route on our return. We skirted the canvas-green artichoke fields, following the two-lane Highway One, the Pacific pacing and snapping beyond the brown cliffs.

The Emmits wanted to stop at the Pigeon Point lighthouse, but the lighthouse was closed. We got out anyway, walked across the ice plants, a variety of ground cover related to cactus. You break off a stub, and it oozes green. We stood watching the ocean, white gulls sprinkling the blue. The lighthouse was not in use as a navigational aid anymore, a sign said. It could be visited between hours which were covered over with a neat rectangle of paper.

Fields along the coast grow flowers for florists, acres of green with color just starting, pastels and half-tones, the blossoms not open yet. As soon as they are about to flower they are gone, shipped to town in plastic tubs. Wooden stands with hand-painted signs offer cherries and strawberries, although the strawberries were gone, now, replaced by olala berries and blackberries, and artichokes, the green thistles Dad steams and eats with butter, or with a special mayonnaise he makes himself.

"Hal and I both agree that therapy is extremely useful," said Mrs. Emmit. She called her husband Hal, my father called him Harold. "A good therapist can do so much." This was Mom-propaganda. I could hear Mom telling her old friend, *Convince her to see Dr. Yellin.*

Mr. Emmit nodded in an overeager way, stepping on the accelerator to pass a truckload of tomatoes.

"Remember that time we all went to see the family therapist?" Mrs. Emmit sang out, over the whine of the engine.

"A nice guy," said Mr. Emmit, doing his part.

A road crew worked a hillside, beyond a sign: CONTROLLED BURN. Black patches seethed blue smoke. Cars backed up, a half hour delay, everyone wanting a look at the few remaining flutters of fire. Devil's Slide, where the highway dips and swerves over land that is always sinking, caving away. Mr. Emmit drove fast, maybe his medication wearing off, the van pitching hard on the curves.

Marta chattered. She wanted to buy an Aqua-Strobe, an underwater flashlight. She said when she had the money and the time she would dive the world, the Solomon Islands, Truk Lagoon. She and her parents tossed the conversational ball back and forth, and although I chimed in with travel stories of my own, Marta did not look my way as she talked.

They refrained from turning on an all-news station,

their favorite kind. The Emmits were delaying on my behalf, back to acting with extreme consideration, wanting to know if I wanted to have a taco—we could stop in the Mission District. Or drive over to Oscar's on Shattuck Avenue for a hamburger.

"Sure," said Marta, not the first time I had sensed envy or jealousy in her voice, "give Wonder Woman whatever she wants."

A code opens the front gate. You push the numerals, Cassandra's birthday and mine, 2/5 and 1/11, and the iron barrier robots open, a motor making a high-pitched whir like an electric pencil sharpener.

The Emmits were already caught up in their own rush to get sheets of masonite for a stage set, and then to Office Depot for some black indelible markers; they had not expected to be back so early in the day.

Already, just taking my time up the driveway, I could see the changes. The fountain had been scrubbed, bleached, or blasted, the tiles that had always been prettily moss green and old world now bright sky blue. Weeds had been cleared from the ivy, and new blue-gray pea gravel tamped around the stepping stones.

I carry my house key on a lime-green coil. The green is supposed to glow in the dark. The door handle had been cleaned, the Marley's-ghost knocker polished bright.

New rugs were in place, deep magentas and iron blues. I could tell it had taken my parents a long time—here, no here—to get the rugs to look casual.

As Mrs. Emmit waved good-bye she had said, "I'll call Ruthie about the interview."

chapter

26

My bedroom was still a vacant lot with a bed in it, but pages of paint swatches were fanned out on the bedspread, along with a furniture catalog and samples of fabric, a book with various shades and textures of cloth.

My dad loves leaving notes. When he can't find anything to write on he uses one of his old business cards, with teeny writing. His note said we could replace the crumby curtains. "How about Tuscan Dawn?" he had written, in such scrunched writing it took a long moment to make it out.

Beside the fat volume of curtain fabrics was an envelope, addressed in Quinn's neat printing. Quinn never writes letters and sometimes doesn't like to exchange even spoken words. People who don't know him think he's either unfriendly or shy.

I was careful with the envelope, because even the plain

white business-size envelope meant something, if only I could understand. Quinn had picked it out.

It was a short letter, but when I had read it I sat down and read it again. Then I folded it and put it in my nightstand. I couldn't let myself think about what it said.

"They arrested him," said Bernice. She said the words with a little denying shake of her head. She didn't like discussing it.

She was in the kitchen, in a big canvas apron, sturdy, like the apron a carpenter might wear.

Sometimes even when you aren't that surprised you stop still for a second.

She said, "It was on the news last night."

She made me a glorious sandwich, smoked trout fillet, Maui onions, and fat slices of tomato. She was packing herbs and spices she bought wholesale in plastic bags into smaller, airtight jars. Cloves, cinnamon sticks, sage.

It wasn't an easy question. "Did they show what he looked like?"

Bernice tilted her head and gave a smile, sheepish, not at all like her. A braid of garlic hung on the wall, beside a wreath of bay leaves.

"They showed a picture," she said, too dignified to say *mug shot.*

How do they know it's him?

"They must have some kind of evidence," I said.

"I'm sure they do," she said, wiping the sink where it didn't need it. Sympathy kept Bernice intent, polishing, selecting a smaller sponge, her hands ever busy.

"What's he look like?" I asked again.

"Older than you would think," she said.

Fat? Skinny? I stopped myself from asking. I guessed at something, needing to know. "Did anything like this ever happen to you?" I asked.

She did not meet my eyes, but it was like she could visualize me perfectly, no need to look. "Like what happened to you the other night?" she asked, although she knew perfectly well.

I told her yes, that's what I meant.

"We all know what it's like," said Bernice.

I knew how the examiner has to ask the same question again, new words, so the interview squeezes out the truth.

But Bernice said, "My problem was medical."

I suddenly didn't want to know any more, not now.

"No, I don't mind telling you." Her emphasis on *you* made me look away.

It took her a moment to find a place on the sink for the sponge. "I used to own a restaurant, called Anisette."

It was a famous eating place, renowned for its desserts. Dad used to take Cass and me there once in a great while for chocolate truffles. Crazily rich candies, black, moist cakes, curls of bittersweet, slabs of white chocolate. Bernice could tell by my eyes that I remembered.

"But one morning I woke up and I couldn't read a balance sheet. I'd go to sign my name on a paycheck, and my hand was making strange letters that didn't mean anything. I would read a book, and the words would fade out in my mind. I couldn't even watch television. Characters would talk, and I didn't hear the sounds as language. The screen was blank to me, except that it had some colored shadows."

A tiny speck of oregano soiled the expanse of white marble where Bernice made pie crust. She cupped one hand and urged the tiny flake toward her palm with the other.

"There was nothing wrong with my eyes," she continued, "or with my powers of perception. Every doctor agreed with the diagnosis that I was depressed." She dusted her hands together, like someone briefly applauding.

A long silence told me that I had to inquire. "Did you get help?"

"I'm getting well. Because of your family."

Dad reads the *Chronicle* inside out, taking it apart, food and sports first, world and East Bay afterward. The newspaper is usually folded, each section, on his desk, before it graduates to a paper bag stuffed with newsprint destined for recycling. But this was a new office, his old oak desk looking distinguished but careworn before a view of the back garden. Scripts for his TV pilot were stacked neatly, "The Ultimate Virgin," all about olive oil, and "Safe-Sex Chocolate," the story of the cocoa bean, from jungle to frosting. A basket held minicassettes, tapes full of ideas.

The newspaper was under the envelope opener, a silver-plated dagger. My hands were cold as I searched the pages. When I found the place where the story of the arrested suspect had been, there was nothing but a hole.

Mom says that silence talks. A prospective employee who never mentions her family or her previous boss is communicating more than she wants to. I could read my father's actions, how he studied the story, and how he took it to L.A. in his pocket.

I changed clothes, into new pants with a label still fluttering and a price tag attached by plastic that would not cut, no matter how I tried. Tuscan Dawn was a "superior latex," the color of bad pancake makeup. I didn't really mind the curtains I had now, coffee-ice-cream off-white.

I put on my running shoes. I pulled the laces tightly through the eyes, tying show-no-mercy knots. I don't like to stop because a lace comes undone.

Quinn's letter said that his father would have trouble leaving the job at the casino, even though he hated it. "Because of a contract he signed long before he knew." Quinn said he would do anything to come be with me, quit school, leave home.

That was the part I couldn't bear to think about, knowing how I had deceived even Quinn.

Mom encourages me to call her pager, "if there's ever a problem." But my mother is someone who hates to be interrupted. I imagined confessing to my mother, shame shutting me up before I even began. I couldn't let myself imagine telling my father, the expression that would fill his eyes.

I hadn't run for a couple of days, and already I felt a couple of phantom pounds around my hips. I found myself heading uphill without thinking, my body knowing exactly where to go. But the slope was punishing, my leg muscles taking a while to warm to the effort. If there is just the tiniest bit of air pollution you feel it center chest, and I forced myself, hard.

I ran, loving the way part of me hated the labor, trying to burn off my feelings like so many fatty calories, loping, long, rhythmic strides. The last of the two-car garages passed, the hillside began, poison oak already scarlet, showing off its color. I ran faster, arms pumping, sweat breaking all over my body.

The pace hurt. And then it stopped hurting, the pain barrier something you leave behind. I crested the hill, saw Sandalwood Ranch ahead, white buildings, dark blue trees. It was down slope just before the tree shade.

Later I would tell myself that I knew I was being followed.

chapter

27

I breathed hard, hanging on to the rails of the corral. The upper half of Desert Flower's stable door was open, but the horse did not answer my whistle. I wasn't surprised. She had never heard it before, and my whistle is pathetic, an airy *thweet.*

The unmarked police car eased along under the eucalyptus.

Detective Margate was wearing a coffee-dark skirt with side pockets, a straw-brown blazer, and looked around at the horsey scenery with a pleasantly interested expression, like she was considering putting a down payment on the place. In this strong afternoon sun her dark hair had hints of auburn. She approached a fan of horse manure, green-gold, without seeing it, eyes on the roof lines and the trees. Sweeping me, too, with her falcon gaze, smiling, saying something.

It took me a moment to recognize the shape of my

name on her lips. Detective Ronert stood beside the car, patting the roof as though it were a large drum, soundlessly, just passing time.

Detective Margate stepped easily over the bright manure, and her Rockports strode through the truck ruts cut into the earth months ago, when there was rain. She put one elbow on a rail.

Tommy Dixon stood on the back step of a freshly painted white office building. He wore a country gentleman outfit today, sports jacket and gray slacks, his thumb hitched in his belt.

I said, "Congratulations."

"Oh, it wasn't our arrest," Detective Margate said breezily.

"But it's over now."

"It can be," she said.

This was one of those statements my Mom calls "smoke." It didn't mean anything, but it was confusing.

I gave myself time. Desert Flower was not making an appearance in the dark square of her stable door.

"Is this where your horse lives?" said the detective, all sweetness.

I had one of those quick certainties, a flash insight. "Did Bernice tell you I was here?" I felt that I should shield Bernice from these two cops, experts at getting information out of people. "Have you been bothering her?"

The detective answered by letting her smile turn thoughtful.

Detective Ronert paddled the car roof, just loud enough. He opened his hands like a catcher anticipating a pitch.

"Let's talk," said Detective Margate.

• • •

Detective Ronert drove, and Detective Margate sat in back, tree shadows streaming across us. The car was traveling fast, all of us leaning as the car cornered, residential streets giving way to storefronts, places that sold fruit smoothies and foreign newspapers.

"That warning light is blinking again," said Detective Ronert. "I'll have to have it checked."

Detective Margate opened a briefcase, pulled out a manila folder, and licked her fingers, the way Dad does using a dictionary. She selected the page she wanted, a garish photo.

I didn't want to take it from her hands. She gave the color photo a shake, *Go on.*

It was a lurid, fleshy blow-up, mottled with blue and tattooed with ruby cuts.

"That's a very interesting picture," the detective was saying. "It took me some time to understand what I was looking at."

"It's my shoulder," I said.

"Exactly. It's you, the night we began our investigation. I want you to look at the bruising."

I gave the picture back to her. She looked at it with the gaze of a proud relative. "Here's another one, a view of your back."

A close up of anyone's skin is surreal, pores like orange rind. The bramble tears were a series of beads, jewels of dried blood in an arc, diminishing to a subtle gash in the skin.

"Where are you taking me?" I asked.

She made a little *that depends* waft of her head, non-

137

committal, but implying that she would take me wherever she wanted. I could see her calculating, despite herself, the way she looked out the window to figure out the right way to express her next thought.

"It's against the law, Jennifer, to file a false police report."

She turned and looked right at me, full face.

"It's a misdemeanor under the California State Penal Code," she said. "Falsely reporting a crime, Section 148.5. Punishable by six months in jail, or imprisonment under the appropriate youth authority. And if you happen to lie under oath—under Penal Code Section 118, that's perjury. A felony."

chapter 28

We pulled into the parking lot of the police station, the cheap motel frame of the building looking even less promising by daylight. A man in a gray jumpsuit was hunched over a car engine, wiping the dipstick with a soiled rag.

Detective Margate went over and said something to the mechanic, her fingers opening and closing, then pointing back at her unmarked car.

I tried to read the posture of Detective Ronert. He held the door, courtly, giving a little bow, as though I were a figure in petticoats and a bonnet.

Detective Margate carried her folder close to her breast, not putting it into her briefcase. The place was exactly like the Department of Motor Vehicles when I got my learner's permit, in/out trays and people in no hurry on the way to the photocopying machine.

Would an innocent person begin to weep? I wondered.

Not me.

I would be angry.

"I had trouble visualizing it from the beginning," she said. "The attacker chased you, ran you down, and put out his hand. He was running along with his arm out. He grabbed your shoulder." She paused meaningfully.

I was sitting in the same comfortable chair with the padded arms. It was upholstered in durable plastic with a mock leather grain. "That's right," I heard my voice say.

"He seized you with his right hand, and you spun, did a three-sixty and hit him."

"In the face."

"The trouble we're having with your story is this. Look at this photo, Jennifer, and this one. They show the bruising on your shoulder, front and back. The bruises are muted, possibly not fresh bruises, but that isn't the problem. I was looking at the evidence all this time and not seeing."

I didn't respond to this silence, and I could tell that my expression was hard for her to read. The pause went on one heartbeat too long.

"This is not the print of a right hand, Jennifer. Look—this is the thumb, very dim, But you can see it." She ran a pencil point along the blue-pink shade in the photo. "This is a left hand."

I waited.

"And the hand is someone my size," she continued. "Look at the width of the print, palm and fingers. This isn't a man's hand, Jennifer."

I didn't have to fake my irritation. I crossed my arms and told myself to stay quiet.

"Do you know what I think, Jennifer?"

I kept my mouth shut.

"I think you filed a false police report to attract attention. I think you did that for a reason we can all sympathize with."

The detective looked at me from under her dark eyebrows. I tried to read what was coming.

"Because," she said, "your mother abuses you."

I was trembling inside, but I don't think it showed in my fingers, my eyes.

"Tell us," said Detective Margate, sitting on the edge of her desk, "what really happened. Explain how it is that a woman's left hand—"

She stopped and leaned forward.

I stared at the floor. The legs of the desk rested in metal coasters so they wouldn't dent the tile.

My throat closed. I shook my head, like someone hit with a skull punch, and nobody moved.

"My mother has never hit me in her life," I said at last.

That was true, almost. I could recall a slap of my hand, reaching for Christmas cookies, pale white star shapes sprinkled with green and red sugar crystals. I could still feel a fervent shake, Mom warning me not to play in the street.

"We contacted a few people at your mother's place of business," said Detective Margate, "and we talked with a couple of former secretaries. Your mother is a woman with a temper."

Detective Ronert's eyes were on me, a track star waiting for the starting pistol.

"Never," I said.

"Explain these pictures to us," said Detective Margate.

A throaty catch in her voice told me how badly she wanted to believe me.

A knock on the door, and someone opened it, a uniformed officer. Detective Margate speared him with a glance, and he backed away, shutting the door carefully.

I felt sick.

"The bruises are from my sister's hand," I said.

"Your sister?" The detective puckered her lips doubtfully. "You let your sister claw you like this?"

"Cass and I have arguments."

"This looks like more than an argument," said Detective Margate, trying to sound matter-of-fact, unable to keep the hope from her voice.

"I said I would do anything to get out of being maid of honor."

The two detectives waited.

"It was in the hall, on the way to my room. She wouldn't let me walk away. She got a hold of me—" Digging her fingers into me, through the cotton of my blouse. Hissing into my ear. Telling me she'd tell Mother that Dad was having an affair with his producer.

I kept my voice steady. "She has a strong grip. I tend to bruise."

"Does your sister get violent with you often?" asked the detective. A new note had entered her voice.

I continued, "The attacker had me for only a second, and I was running hard. I was wearing a sweatshirt with thick cloth, and he didn't have half of Cass's intensity."

I was looking at the floor, but I could sense the two detectives locking glances.

"Has your sister ever sought help?" asked the detective.

"Cass is studying psychology," I said. Cass had never had a moment of doubt, never an instant of stage fright.

"Your family doesn't intervene?"

"Intervene in what?" I said.

"My brothers and I were always horsing around," said Detective Ronert after a silence. "Maybe it's not a big deal. Kids get hurt."

Detective Margate fumbled through her folder and found what she wanted.

I had thought this would be over now, the bruises explained, everybody happy.

As she extended her hand I caught a glimpse of her wedding band, rose-gold, and an engagement ring, a small diamond. I wondered what she told her husband about her work, and what it would be like if she had children, how she would explain her job to them.

"This won't be a surprise. You've had a look at this already," she said. "On the news."

I did not want to see, but it was too late.

chapter 29

A man's face gazed out of a mug shot, full color, a weary, harried expression, before an ascending line of ruled marks along the margin, indicating his height. He was five feet nine inches tall. It was a stare that almost appeared wise, a runner after a losing marathon. He had lost, but he had finished. He looked like the composite drawings in the news, but more gaunt, as though he strained to keep in shape. His features were powder-puffed with rose and blue markings.

"The officers involved used excessive zeal," said Detective Margate.

"Why did they arrest him?"

"He has a good alibi for the night he attacked you," said Detective Margate. "He can name witnesses, friends he was with in a Chinese restaurant in San Lorenzo."

His left cheek was bruised, right where my fist would have struck it.

"Why is he in jail?" I asked.

"All the other attacks were in a distinct geographical area. Look here." She shook out a map of the East Bay, and a blue X marked locations in East Oakland, near the zoo, in San Leandro near the hills.

"The attack on you was several miles north of his territory."

"He was wearing a ski mask."

"Recognizing his face doesn't matter," said Detective Margate.

"You can look at him all you want," Detective Ronert chimed in, relaxed, now, hands in his pockets. "His facial features are public knowledge."

"Why did they arrest him?" I insisted.

"We can't discuss the case in detail," said Detective Margate. "We can't tell you why he is a suspect. But without your help, this man will be out of jail this time tomorrow."

I held the mug shot out to her, and when she didn't take it immediately it fell, spinning to the floor.

"I can't do it," I said.

"Oakland Police are making a tape of his voice according to the script we've created. You won't have to see him, or be in his presence. You'll sit in a room like this—" She gestured, a realtor showing off a room with a stunning decor.

"A little bigger," offered Detective Ronert.

"The suspect's attorney will be there," she continued. "And one of your parents or their representative, an attorney or a counselor, should be there with you. We'll be there, too, Dave and I. We're on your side, Jennifer. And we'll have Duncan Pierce along, too, the forensic psychologist. We're your friends."

Detective Ronert blinked, acknowledging all this.

"It won't be difficult, Jennifer," she said.

"I won't."

"You'll listen to a tape of various voices. You will say which voice sounds most like him. You'll be able to take as long as you need."

"No."

She didn't move or make a sound right away.

"That's fine," she said finally, putting a pencil back in the holder on her desk, a Berkeley Police coffee mug stuffed with writing implements. "You've convinced us. The strain will be too great. We'll drive you home. You've been very cooperative. Dave, go on down and see if the car's ready."

When he had gone, she told me, confidingly, "The red *oil* alarm keeps blinking." She made that gesture with her fingers again, a motion like a bird's beak opening, shutting, showing how the light flashed. "We keep topping it off with multigrade. I think it must be an electrical short. A burned out fuse under the dash. What do you think?"

I almost told her that I didn't know that much about cars, but I recognized the tactic, *Get her talking about anything and she's hooked.*

"I was sure you were protecting your mother," she said. "And now I see that you're protecting yourself."

I already missed Detective Ronert.

"You're going to cooperate with us, Jennifer. I'll show you why."

• • •

She didn't have to tell me that these women were dead. Photo after photo, in lurid color, the faces of women looking sodden, people plunging out of depths for a gasp of air, unable to open their mouths.

I stayed in my fake leather chair, files open in my lap, spilling onto the floor. I tried not to focus too hard on the images, protecting myself. The pictures trembled in my hands.

"Our suspect didn't do these women," she said. She used *do* in a flat, vile way. "These are other cases, rape and murder, open files, technically. But we'll never find who committed these crimes, Jennifer. These voices cannot speak."

I stopped looking, closing a folder. The thought swept through me: I could tell Detective Margate everything, now. I wrestled to convince myself that the truth would be easier than this.

"Here in this cardboard box I have old files, more open cases, rape victims, no arrest ever made. We have a fallout shelter here at the police station, left over from the Cold War. We use it as storage for old, unsolved crimes, and the place is packed. This is why I'm a detective, Jennifer. I could make better money selling insurance, like my sister Julie. I could teach school, like my mother."

I tried to imagine Detective Margate in a wedding dress, in white satin Kenneth Cole footwear.

"I wouldn't talk like this in front of Dave. Men don't like it when you get emotional. It makes them nervous. Dave's a good detective, though, so I thought I'd spare him the pain of watching you aiding and abetting a criminal. Hindering an investigation."

I tried to imagine her with friends, deciding she'd have a piece of the whiskey chocolate cake.

"You can walk out of here and let us give you a ride home, but I'll never forget you, Jennifer. I'm coming after you, week after week. I'll send you clippings of the rapes and brutal attacks this criminal makes on other women, Jennifer. That's why you'll be a witness against this felon. I'm not giving you any choice."

chapter

30

After the fluorescent light of the police department, the late afternoon sun was heirloom gold, and our shadows fell ahead of us over the parking spaces carefully designated with yellow stripes.

The unmarked car had been washed, filmy towel swipes drying on the windshield. Detective Ronert drove, and I sat in the front seat, my knee against the empty shotgun bracket on the dash.

"It's still broken," said Detective Ronert.

Detective Margate, leaning over from the back seat, didn't say anything. I couldn't keep myself from looking.

Oil kept flashing red.

"Jennifer, tomorrow we'll pick you up in one of our new Chevies," said Detective Ronert. "Tinted glass in the back. Our prime-witness car. We'll impress the hell out of the Oakland police."

They dropped me off at Animal Heaven at my request. I wasn't supposed to come in that afternoon, and neither was Marta. Mr. DaGama was glad to see me, telling me the African Gray had made a noise that morning that sounded just like me.

"What did he say?"

"The actual word was hard to understand," said Mr. Da Gama, working a twenty-pound bag of wild bird seed into a paper sack. "But it was your voice."

Byron was hanging by his beak from the side of his cage, eyeing me as I approached. Without disconnecting his beak, he made a chuckling, ripped-steel noise, loud enough to stop me in my tracks.

A happy parrot is generally noisy, cackling, yelling. I picked a peanut from an open bag of East Bay Pet Whole-sale seed, selecting a fine, fat one, and all the birds began to sound off, each wanting food and attention.

Byron accepted the peanut and then had to negotiate his cage, all the way down to his perch, without dropping it from his hooked beak. He clambered, inch by inch, offering a muttering, pleased discourse with me and with the other birds. And maybe with the peanut, too, telling the goober how tasty it looked. At last he gripped the peanut in one foot and unhusked it with his beak, his pupils dilating wildly, vibrant with pleasure.

I fed them all, made sure dishes were overflowing with seed, cleaned out the cages.

I waved good-bye to Mr. Da Gama, who was on the phone and could only give me a military-style salute in farewell.

I went home.

• • •

I watched the Discovery Channel in my bedroom. The bones of a mammoth were discovered by dam builders. A jazz pianist looked back on his forty-year career. Hummingbirds migrated from Oregon to Mexico, using the same landmarks used by human pilots, Mt. Shasta, San Francisco Bay. I propped myself on pillows but made no attempt to sleep, riding out the night with the TV remote in my hand, until nearly three in the morning.

The street outside was still.

Sometimes the quietest sounds carry best. I could hear the subtle open-and-shut of cupboards, the faraway shuffling, all but inaudible.

He was in the kitchen, at the breakfast counter with a bowl in front of him and a large spoon.

He tucked his head when he saw me, with a hand-in-the-cookie jar grin, and said, "Bernice made her special ice cream. I'm sorry you weren't feeling well."

My reflection flowed across the chrome toaster, restaurant quality, enough slots for ten slices of toast at once.

"Your mom and I couldn't put a dent in it," Dad was saying. "I just couldn't resist, lying there, knowing it was in the fridge."

Mom had spend a half hour on the phone before supper with Detective Margate, Mom wandering from room to room with the portable telephone. She kept agreeing, saying, "Yes, I see," sounding gradually more and more fatigued.

In the end all my mother had said to me was, "Jennifer, at least I'll be there with you," in one of those dramatically weary tones she uses to silence argument. Mother would have killed before she let Cass go through an ordeal with the police.

I helped myself to the big tub in the freezer, a cardboard container big enough to hold a human head, packed with ivory billows of vanilla ice cream. I topped it with chocolate syrup and sprinkled salted peanuts on it, as Dad looked on approvingly. The syrup was cold and poured out thick, oozing out of the Hershey's can, slowly descending to the ice cream.

"That's why a very wise scientist invented the microwave," said Dad, hunched on his stool. "It wasn't just so you could reheat a whole cup of coffee in ten seconds."

I could hear Cass in my mind, telling me to go ahead and ask. She would know: I didn't have the nerve.

chapter

31

Pots hung from hooks, casting vague shadows over the sink, the yellow Dualit toaster, the jars of dried herbs. The oversize fridge fell silent—a sound I was aware of as soon as it stopped.

The opening question is very important. It sets the tone every other question builds on. "You've been busy in L.A.," I said.

Dad lifted his shoulder, let it fall, a gesture I use all the time. "I do the same thing over and over. Standing under these hot TV lights. I say, 'Polenta is corn meal cooked on the stove, stirred lovingly with a wooden spoon.' And then I do it again. I say, 'with a *wooden* spoon', and next time I say, 'stirred *lovingly.*' The same words, a different emphasis."

The ice cream made my teeth ache. I usually love it. I sat at the kitchen table, looking over at my father. We were two diners in a spacious late-night coffee shop.

"And pretty soon the words are nonsense syllables," he continued. "I'm getting my picture taken today," he said. "I'm going to look awful. I should be upstairs asleep, or lying quiet with ice cubes on my eyes."

"Why do you need another picture of your face?"

"For full-page ads, me holding the new Ultra-Lo Ranch Dressing."

"Reschedule the photo session," I suggested.

"Thanks, Jenny. A lot. You're telling me I look like doggy-doo."

He looked like a tired man eating ice cream in his bathrobe. Although he said he had leased a convertible in L.A., he didn't have much of a tan.

"Cass told me something," I said. I was wearing a bathrobe I rarely put on, a rose satin wraparound with Belgian lace frills, big pockets. It was the sort of thing you'd wear if you had a silver cigarette case and called your makeup space a boudoir.

I had begun, and I couldn't unsay it.

But when I didn't continue immediately, Dad said, dryly, "Well, that's unusual—Cass having something to talk about." Unlike Mom, Dad sometimes caught the expression in Cass's eyes when she was charming someone on the phone, accepting yet another compliment.

"It was about how things were going for you down in L.A."

He shoveled ice cream into his mouth.

"She mentioned you and Maggie," I said.

Dad made a little, noncommittal "Mmm?"

"Cass said you and Maggie are having an affair."

The spoon stopped midway to his mouth. His hand felt for a napkin, found it, and he wiped his lips.

"Cass said this?"

"Yes," I said.

He said, "She was joking."

"She threatened to tell Mom."

He ran a thumb over his eyebrows. He was quiet for a long time.

"I keep hoping we'll see improvement," he said at last. "As Cass matures. But I'm still continually surprised."

Ice cream is terrible for the human voice, cools the vocal cords and coats them with milk phlegm. I cleared my throat, took my time, and asked, "Are you saying that it's not true?"

Dad had been staring at his empty spoon, like someone trying to make out his reflection. He peered at me. "You don't believe it!"

My voice was barely above a whisper, so I stopped trying to talk.

"This is very disturbing," he said. "Very troubling." He acted the way people do when they get bad news, expressing their surprise, not absorbing it.

I shifted my fingers slightly on the counter.

"Cass saying it is one thing," he said. "But, Jennifer, the thought of you believing it—"

The corner of the kitchen embraced a large brick fireplace with pothooks and a stack of pristine firewood. The fireplace had been obsolete when the house was built, but it radiated imaginary warmth. Dad got off his stool and came around the counter toward me, like a compact bruin in his dark blue bathrobe. Something about me stopped him, and he turned toward the fireplace, moving at half speed, his new leather slippers sticking very slightly to the floor with each step.

He spoke as though to the uncharred oakwood. "Cassandra said—what were her words, exactly?"

"That's what she said."

"What, exactly?" he asked impatiently

I couldn't bring myself to say it again.

"It's a threat, isn't it? She's going to tell Elizabeth this story."

I said, "Cass won't tell her."

"Why not?" He came back to the breakfast counter and put his hands flat on the surface. "What's going to keep Cassandra from saying anything that crawls into her head?"

"I gave in."

"You 'gave in'—and agreed to what?"

"I agreed that I wouldn't change my mind about being maid of honor."

"This is how you and your sister talk? How you plan the wedding?" He picked up his bowl and padded across the kitchen to the stainless steel vault of the kitchen sink. He ran water into the bowl longer than he had to.

Mom says you don't have to answer every question, pick and choose.

"Do you know what I found the other night," he said, "when I was putting my Dickens up on the bookshelves? I found one of your mother's tape cassettes, from music school. And you know what I did?" This was a little unusual for my father, advancing question by question. "I put on a pair of earphones and listened to her tear Carmen to pieces. Glorious singing. A beautiful voice."

He wasn't saying it never happened.

"I used earphones, because you know how your mother would react if she heard the sound of her singing."

He was not calling it a lie.

"She'd tell me to please turn it off," he said. "She'd be embarrassed. This beautiful sound she could make—and she was embarrassed even years ago. Always. Even when I first heard her in that apartment I rented downstairs from her on Parker Street. And went up to her door with a plate of pound cake I had just baked."

He dried his hands and folded the towel, and he was preparing himself as he created a neat square of terry cloth, getting ready.

"It's not true, Jennifer," he said. "Cass was telling a lie."

The delay in making a denial. The show of exasperated weariness, the patient overemphasis, the way he spaced out the words. I weighed the sound of his voice, his choice of words. He steadied his gaze, forced it, calm, sincere.

I wasn't sure I could believe him.

chapter 32

I tiptoed along the hall, letting the bathroom door breathe open. But the robe made a flouncy rustle, and I went slowly, my arms wrapped around my sides, approaching the medicine cabinet like someone who wasn't really there.

Dad had to make a decision, whether to go back to bed or stay up and catch an earlier flight. He had made coffee, poured the shiny French roast beans into the electric grinder, and as I left the kitchen he said, "I'll call you."

He made me respond to him, saying, "Jennifer, I'll give you a call," until I nodded: Message received.

The pill vials were all childproof. I had to press down on each lid and turn, dumping the contents into my pockets. The label on these pills was new, refills remaining, two, Dr. Rigby's old pill containers lined up like chess pieces in an old sterile gauze box.

I emptied all the pills I could find, each plastic cylinder, into my elegant-courtesan dressing gown. When my pockets bulged, the pills made a chalky, calcium grind with each step, like crushed bone, and the satin slithered and whispered all the way to my bedroom.

I placed the voice-activated tape recorder on the edge of my desk.

A red light comes on when you make a sound. Picking up the recorder and moving it to the nightstand, where it is less likely to tumble, made the light come on just as surely as my voice.

I told them where I would be, where I knew brush and trees provided a secluded location. I wanted to be close to where people came and went, on the margin, but not so far away no one would ever find what was left.

I puzzled over what to wear. I rolled on some scentless Ban. I don't approve of shaving my legs, but I do it anyway, with a Phillips electric. I took time, up and down my legs with the twin rotary head, the batteries starting to weaken. A backpack would be cumbersome, and even the sportiest purse was out of the question. Cass had given me a fanny pack one Christmas, Italian leather, but I never felt right running down the street with a bulge full of Kleenex and coins herniating out of my back. I think that was why Cass gave it to me, a practical, casual item Cass herself was too smart to wear.

So I slipped into running pants with deep zipper pockets, and a soft cotton sash between loops. The pockets bulged when I emptied all the pills into them and zipped them up, so I put on an oversize silk jacket over my Cal sweatshirt with the cutoff sleeves. It was a remnant of my roomy wardrobe, when everything I bought was big enough for a heavyweight wrestler. I tucked my hair up under a watch cap, but it looked too mean-streets for this dawn. I shook out my hair, brushed it, and held it with a blue plastic clasp.

I didn't forget a little paper money, held together with a large pink plastic paper clip. I laced on my shoes, and then found myself holding the little Sony recorder.

The recorder kept turning off and on every time I tapped my fingernails on the desk or made the noise Dad makes, a throat-clearing cough, the noise an animal might make, letting the other elk know where he is. I set the tape recorder to manual and switched it on.

I was going to tell everything, but I saw my parents in my mind, unable to comprehend what they were hearing. I saw Quinn when he heard the truth, stunned, bitter, knowing I had deceived everyone I knew.

And Cass—playing the tape over and over again in secret, trying to keep Danny from finding out what her sister was really like.

I couldn't begin to say the words.

I made the bed, something one of Bernice's helpers would not have to do, and tucked the minicassette under the pillowcase, where I left it barely visible, a plastic gleam surrounded by mercerized cotton.

I posed myself from place to place in the room, the way Mom does.

By now I was nervous.

• • •

Birds were in the trees, claiming their territory, letting every other bird know a twig on Planet Earth was fully occupied. It's a happy sound even when you know how hungry they are, after a night without feeding.

You hear about yogis, adept at meditation, how they sit for hours letting nothingness console their soul, fill them up. It's impossible, you think. No one can just empty themselves and sit in silence. But that is what I did. I sat on the edge of the bed until sun filled the pleated curtains.

Dad's Lincoln was already purring down the driveway on his way out when I peeked. He ran the windshield wipers, approaching the gate. Sometimes a car looks like a living beast, hesitating, forging ahead.

I tucked the cassette with its message of where they could find me into the toe of one of the satin sling-backs, my maid-of-honor shoes.

chapter

33

My mother's shower door makes a muted growl in its metal track, another domestic sound I would never get used to.

She takes two kinds of showers, a quick rinse and dry and long, muscle kneading interludes. I hurried. I had to pause on the front steps to tighten my laces. My hands had been numb, and I had not pulled the laces tight the first time. Bernice's car waited as the front gate creaked open on her way to work, her headlights on even though it was full daylight now.

Bernice is one of those people who say *Good morning* first thing, never *Hello*. She mouthed the words through the window of her Mazda, and I said, "Hi."

I sensed her eyes following me, her car taking a moment before it scooted up the driveway, a whiff of car exhaust in the air.

I made it through the gate before the one-horsepower

motor closed it, but I didn't start running right away. The dozens of pills in my zipper pockets felt like twin bean-bags, and the floppy silk jacket flowed around me, confining even at a fast walk. I strode briskly up Campus Drive, power-walking past the sleepy, brown-shingle Victorians and the multi-unit apartments made out of white, grandmotherly houses.

I popped into a convenience store, the kind of place that sells computer software and ready-made sandwiches. I bought a half-pint of orange juice, the only size they had. I went back for another bottle when I realized it wasn't nearly enough fluid, and the clerk put them into a plastic bag.

I would follow the jogging trail, and when I reached the place—there my plan ran out of script. I thought I would ease myself—not rolling, not stumbling this time—down the bank of blackberry thorns, and sit within the sound of cars and joggers and take the pills, one by one.

I pried the cap off a plastic bottle of Berkeley Farms orange juice, "from concentrate," and as I walked along, the juice splashed out onto my hand. It was cold and, after a half block or so, sticky. I stopped, put the unopened bottle in its flutter of plastic bag on the curb.

I unzipped my pocket and placed two tablets on my tongue. I washed them down with a swallow of breathtakingly cold juice.

chapter

34

It did not take me long, accompanied by the whisk and blast of morning traffic, to realize that swallowing these pain pills would take ages. So I put a few more in my mouth and swallowed, determined to hold off on ingesting the majority until I had reached my destination. But it was a challenge to stop, take pills, swallow, with bicyclists whirring by, the supply of orange juice running out way before the pills.

I found myself observing my hand, palm wrinkles cupping dazzling white pills, stuffing the quantities into my mouth. I sipped the juice, not taking great gulps, conserving. The pills went down hard, and even harder when I tried swallowing them naked, without any juice at all.

I gagged. I dropped the empty orange juice container into a green plastic-only bin, and stuffed the bag in after it.

Tennis players drilled each other on a concrete court. No amiable serves, no easygoing returns. They were practicing kill-shots. I felt good. Alert, observant, thankful that I had chosen such a fresh morning.

The pills were weak. The medicine had conquered my headache, I recalled, after a prolonged fight. The power of this stuff was exaggerated. My stomach was awash in pills and juice, and I felt only the slightest tingle in my lips. Cars squealed to a stop, a traffic light, a red hand ordering me to stay where I was. A couple of men in summer-weight tweeds looked at me, up and down. I get attention like this only when I wear running clothes.

A man with a shopping cart full of mashed beer cans was trudging against the traffic. He was dressed like I was, except that his outfit was well broken-in. He wore a zipper jacket, his running pants dirty at each knee, his running shoes worn toeless. His hair was carefully parted, but had the shiny, clogged appearance of hair that needs to be shampooed.

The man smiled the way Mr. Emmit sometimes does, a cheerful grimace of effort, and I hurried with my orange juice, coughing down one fistful of pills after another. I wanted him to have my empty bottle.

It was a struggle but I was ready for him as he passed, and he caught my bottle with one hand, almost dropped it, tossed into his shopping cart, and gave me a flash of his teeth. I wanted to tell him that there was another empty container in the recycling bin not far away, but for the first time I began to think that the medication might possibly be having some influence on my thoughts.

It was subtle, but maybe the pills did have power, after all.

chapter

35

My fingertips tingled, and my feet struck the ground flat, not in that graceful heel/toe stroke of the ground you take for granted. It was funny, in an ugly way. My feet plodded along, my arms hanging slack, my hands lead pendulums at the end of my bones.

Cyclists shifted gears, the ratcheting sound accompanying the pronounced gristly leverage of the knees as they glided past. I sat on the curb, shivering, the air around me ice.

I told myself that it was very smart for me to take a seat beside a bus stop and reflect, because I was feeling very weary. The bus stop bench was made of concrete, gray cement with fine bubbles in it, gray cheese. I leaned my head against it. I was very tired, completely exhausted, and my eyes slipped shut.

I opened them slowly, one eye out of focus until I blinked hard.

When you sit down and watch a motorcycle putter exhaust into the morning air, all the things you have been doing become clear. It's easy, then, like someone squeezing frosting onto a cake, to see a spot you have missed. Birds bickered in the bushes behind me, and in the date palm over my head.

When my eyes eased shut again I could hear where the palm fronds ended and the empty sky began. I could imagine my father, asking what kind of birds they were. I could hear Cass saying they were slum birds, sparrows.

I had not expected to feel like this. I wrapped my arms around myself, like someone falling, downward through space.

I swung to my feet.

People make the gesture jokingly—they stick a finger in their mouths and make a face like throwing up. But I thrust my finger all the way past my soft palate and into my glottal region, and nothing happened. My hand tasted vaguely of salt and a little orange juice.

I squinted at the sun to determine the correct direction. The concrete was a wilderness of cracks, white and yellow grass worn to nubs in the fissures.

I ran hard, and stumbled. My skin abraded painlessly on the curb, blood welling from a dozen minute sources in my flesh. I found my stride again, a loping, long distance pace, no sensation in my lips, my tongue. As long as I kept moving, life would pump through my arms and my legs, but if I slowed down for even a moment, to ask for help, to call 911 at a pay phone, all of this would disappear.

I kept the pace, running hard in the direction I believed

was home. A tart, bad-milk phlegm filled my mouth. Sounds faded, and ceased. There was no noise, nothing.

Not even the sawing of my breath.

When I found the pay phone I had trouble pushing the O for operator. My finger kept crooking, my finger slipping off the button.

I could barely hear the phone trilling in my ear.

When a distant voice said, "Thank you for using A T and T," and asked if she could help me, I felt the danger, how the impersonally polite voice could misunderstand my silence, in a hurry to respond to other callers, other people she would never know.

I spoke, and the words came out clumsy, my tongue fat. I had to begin to tell my story.

And I had trouble shaping words.

She understood just enough of what I said. "Is this an emergency?" she was asking.

Time was running out on me, on what I had to say. I said, "I have to speak to the Berkeley Police."

"Is this an emergency?" she was insisting.

"Sex Crimes Detail," I said to the male voice that answered the phone. "I need Detective Margate."